C000016992

UNTIL TOMORROW

Sandra Steffen

A KISMET® Romance

METEOR PUBLISHING CORPORATION
Bensalem, Pennsylvania

KISMET® is a registered trademark of Meteor Publishing Corporation

Copyright © 1993 Sandra E. Steffen
Cover Art Copyright © 1993 Laurence Schwinger

All rights reserved.

No part of this book may be reproduced, stored in a retrieval system, or transmitted in any form, by any means, including mechanical, electronic, photocopying, recording or otherwise, without prior written permission of the publisher, Meteor Publishing Corporation, 3369 Progress Drive, Bensalem, PA 19020.

First Printing May 1993.

ISBN: 1-56597-060-8

All the characters in this book are fictitious. Any resemblance to actual persons, living or dead, is purely coincidental.

Printed in the United States of America.

For my sons, Greg, Doug, Brad, and Mike.
You make me laugh, you make me proud,
you keep me humble.

SANDRA STEFFEN

Sandra Steffen grew up in Michigan, surrounded by an extremely large, noisy family where the changing seasons couldn't help but inspire romance. She doesn't know where she acquired her love of books, but remembers happy hours spent reading as a child. That love of reading transformed into a love of writing several years ago. She, her husband, and their four school age sons live within miles of that large, noisy family, which has become larger and noisier than ever.

Other books by Sandra Steffen:

No. 90 *HOLD BACK THE NIGHT*

ONE

"Was that a truck I heard?"

This was the third time Mara had asked that question and the third time Bekka shook her head. "You said you didn't drop in just because Conor Bradley happens to be delivering my blueprints this afternoon."

Mara didn't answer, and Bekka's gaze followed her sister's, whose attention was now fixed on a portrait that had been taken over five years ago, when Jimmy and Jason had been babies. In the photograph Bekka held her sons protectively on her lap. Mara was looking not at the boys, but at their father, who stood behind them, aloof and uncomfortable even then.

"Remember what you said after Ted's funeral, Bek? Just before you left Cincinnati and came home?" Mara asked. "You said Ted was your biggest mistake. Honestly, Bekka, you swore he'd be your last."

"I meant it."

"Then why do you want to hire Conor Bradley to remodel your kitchen?"

Bekka crossed her arms and raised her chin. She'd made up her mind, and no one, not even her sister

7

whom she loved dearly, was going to change it. "I've seen his work. He's good, Mar, and his company's was the lowest bid."

"Of course his was the lowest bid! Hoodlums can't charge as much as reputable carpenters."

"I don't believe Conor was ever as bad as everyone said. Besides, that was a long time ago," Bekka reminded her sister.

"But he set fire to his own house!"

Bekka didn't raise her voice but laced it with a warning. "That fire was investigated. Anything connecting Conor to it was a rumor and you know how I feel about rumors." Her gaze returned to the portrait, to the handsome man who, for a short time, had been her husband. "Everyone deserves a second chance."

"Oh, Bekky, when are you going to stop blaming yourself for what happened to Ted?"

Instead of answering, Bekka turned away from the photograph and her sister's expectant gaze. She was aware of the deep breath Mara took and the way she clamped her mouth shut in resignation.

"Everyone says you're the patient one. Hah! I always knew you were more stubborn than me. You're just quiet about it, and I'm . . ."

"Not." Bekka spoke the word softly, finishing her sister's statement before leading the way into her old kitchen and away from talk of rumors and heartaches and vague memories of a man she hardly knew, memories as dim as a forgotten dream.

Conor Bradley applied his foot to the brake as the old truck bucked over the gravel country road. His left hand automatically groped along the door for the handle to lower the window. An instant later warm air lifted his hair from his forehead, where worries crowded through his mind, worries of deadlines and materials and half his construction crew out with the flu.

The sight of the house in the distance momentarily chased those worries away. Old houses fascinated him; the sprawling Victorians built in the previous century, the classically simple Americanas with their spare two-story design, and the old cabins with their rustic exteriors and stark interiors. But old brick houses were his favorite. Conor had never been sure whether it was due to an architectural style or to the fact that bricks didn't burn.

This one was a beauty, its country setting serene, peaceful. It was the type of house where families lived, the kind with flower boxes and white curtains, shade trees, and bicycles left in the driveway. It was the kind of house whose nearest neighbor was half a mile away, and it was the exact opposite of the house he'd grown up in.

A tractor was lumbering down a lane across the road as Conor pulled into the driveway, curved around an old oak tree, and threw the lever into park in front of the garage. Tucking the blueprints beneath his arm, he slid from the seat and took the porch steps two at a time. He punched the doorbell and pulled his fingers through his hair, trying to rouse a dose of patience. Patience had never been his strong suit, and today was no exception.

Voices, too faint to be understood, carried on the breeze. Conor muttered under his breath and pressed the bell again, listening for the resounding chime inside. Realizing the bell wasn't working, he rattled his fist against the glass pane. Silence replaced feminine voices. A lacy curtain was ruffled and a woman with eyes as blue as the Michigan sky opened the door.

"I'm Conor Bradley, from Pearson Construction Company."

"I know."

To his surprise, the woman smiled, and Conor felt the softness of her smile all the way down to his knees. She leaned forward and took the blueprints from his hand. "I'm Bekka Stevenson. Won't you come in?"

He followed her inside, his gaze dropping from her dark blond hair down to the proud set of her shoulders and the feminine sway of her hips. He wondered how she'd known him. Had she been a classmate? He didn't think so. He swore he'd have remembered that smile.

"This is my sister, Mara . . ."

"You haven't changed a bit, Conor." At first glance the woman who'd spoken could have been Bekka's double. But on closer inspection he noticed the subtle differences, the slight roundness of her cheeks, the darker shade of her hair. For a moment her blue eyes held none of the warmth Bekka's had. Then she laughed, and Conor was amazed at the change. "You don't remember me, do you?"

He kicked his professionalism into high gear. "I'm afraid not. I've been away a long time."

"I was three years behind you in school, but I dated Vince Macelli a few times. My father and brothers were ready to lock me in the attic . . ."

"Mara!" Bekka admonished.

"Well, they were! Conor Bradley and Vince Macelli, what a pair you two were. Believe me, *all* the girls knew you."

A familiar tension crawled down Conor's spine. After all this time he should have been used to it. But a reputation, especially a bad one, was hard to live down.

Bekka handed one end of the blueprints to her sister. "Mar, help me open this up."

Mara spread out her end, but it didn't deter her conversation. "I'll never forget the night you left, the night your house burned to the ground. We could see the flames, smell the smoke from home over a mile away. It seemed the wail of those sirens could be heard from here to eternity. All that was left the next morning was rubble and ashes. I was . . .''

"Just leaving," Bekka stated, taking the print from her sister's hands.

"I was?"

Conor saw Bekka nod, the kind of nod that left no room for argument. As she escorted Mara to the door, Mara sputtered, "Are you crazy, Bek? You know there's strength in numbers."

Even though she'd whispered, the words reached Conor's ears like taunts. For a moment the old anger came crashing through his body, nearly blinding him with visions of the past, until he felt like the seventeen-year-old boy he'd been. *Bradley, keep your mind on business.*

He needed a vacation. Hell, he'd needed one all his life. Raking his fingers through his hair, he tried to tramp down the old feelings of anxiety and defeat. When his vision cleared, he found himself staring into Bekka's serene blue eyes.

"Sometimes Mara says things she shouldn't." Though her voice was soft, it was more of a grumble than an apology, and Conor could think of nothing to say in return. His pulse jumped and his body drew tight. In the weeks he'd been back, hard work had exhausted him, mind and body. But hard work hadn't prepared him for the tenderness in her gaze.

His own gaze dropped from her eyes to her mouth. Her lips parted slowly. Just as slowly, his gaze trailed back to hers. He'd bet his last meal he wasn't the only one who felt the sensual pull. Bekka felt it, too, but she wasn't giving in to the atmosphere. Raising her chin, she broke eye contact and led the way into the old country kitchen.

"I've been saving the kitchen for last," she confessed. "It's the only room downstairs left to redo. I had all the windows replaced last year, the living and dining rooms remodeled the year before."

Conor liked the way she spoke, direct and concise one minute, smooth and sultry the next. She lifted her gaze to his, and for a moment the fog in his memories cleared. He remembered staring into those same blue eyes, remembered a vague kindness, but didn't remember the time or the place. Had he known her before? Something about her called to the restlessness deep inside him. For some reason it seemed this wasn't the first time.

Getting down to business, he slid a small pad and pencil from his shirt pocket and began jotting down sizes and materials, checking the blueprint periodically.

He smoothed his hand over molding, absently caressing the wide trim that curved around an arched doorway. "You have a beautiful home."

"This place is my life's passion, this house and my children. Not necessarily in that order, of course."

"Kids?"

"Two boys. Nearly six and seven."

He swallowed hard. Of course she'd have kids. A woman like her would want a houseful of them. Too bad. He would have liked to get to know her better. Conor knew next to nothing about women like her, even less about children.

Footsteps echoed over the hollow porch floor and a screen door slammed as two young boys burst through the hall and into the spacious kitchen. One boy was barely an inch taller than the other and no more than half a step ahead.

"Mom, there's a truck parked in the driveway . . ."

the boys said simultaneously, quieting the moment they noticed the stranger standing in their path.

"Jimmy, Jason, this is Conor Bradley from the construction company. He's going to begin work on the kitchen. Mr. Bradley, my sons, Jimmy and Jason."

She had stepped between the two children, and if a voice could smile, hers would be doing just that. Conor watched her place a slender hand on each boy's shoulder. With a yearning called back from his own childhood, a knot coiled in his stomach.

Conor hadn't been around little kids in a long time. He could barely remember how to act around them. Who was he trying to fool? He'd never known how to act around kids, not even when he was a kid himself.

The younger child peered up at him with a mischievous grin. "Doesn't Santa have a reindeer named Conor?"

"That's Donner, you dummy!" the older boy taunted.

"I'm not dumb. You're dumb!"

"Boys, neither of you is dumb. And I don't want you to talk to one another like that," Bekka reprimanded.

Both pairs of eyes were suddenly fixed on the scuffed toe of their shoes. "Okay, Mom," the older boy whispered.

"Okay, Mommy," the other one chided. "Can me and Jimmy watch Conan the Barbarian now?"

Bekka nodded and the child grinned up at Conor. "That's me and Jimmy's favorite cartoon!"

On their way out of the room, the smaller child said, "Conor and Conan sound the same."

"Does not."

"Does so."

"Does not."

Bekka leaned against the old counter. In a voice laced with indulgence, she said, "I hope you'll excuse my children. I'm afraid they have a terribly straightforward approach. I keep hoping they'll outgrow it.''

Her ease in dealing with the situation amazed him and helped put him at ease. Standing opposite Bekka, he brought his hand to the back of his neck and said, ''My name's been a source of attack for as long as I can remember. I'll never forget the time in the second grade when an eleven-year-old bully named Buzz loosened my front tooth while I was defending my name and honor. I don't know what ever inspired my mother to name me Conor.''

''An eleven-year-old second-grader?''

Conor nodded and stared wordlessly at the warmth glimmering in her eyes. The tenderness repeated in her smile snuck up on him, curling into his chest, dropping lower.

''Your mother chose your name?''

Her simple question wiped away what could have been his first smile in days. ''Yeah.'' His name was all his mother had ever given him.

''Conor—'' Bekka's voice had gone as soft as her smile. ''I like that name, but believe me, I know how brutal kids can be. My second-grade students are sometimes horrible to one another.''

As if realizing how she sounded, she took a deep breath, returning her voice to normal. ''Mr. Bradley, when will someone from your company begin work on my kitchen?''

''Conor,'' he said abruptly. ''Please, call me Conor. We're running a little behind, but I plan to be out here early next week.''

Just because she'd said she liked his name was no reason for a hot ache to rise to his throat. He was finished with what he'd come here to do, yet he was reluctant to leave. There was something about this house, something about this woman. He was already hours behind in his work, days behind, but he wanted to linger. Too bad she had children. Too bad he had absolutely no idea how to relate to children. Too bad.

"I'm looking forward to getting this remodeling project finished," Bekka said, walking ahead of him toward the front door.

"I'm looking forward to getting it started," he replied, clearing the lump from his throat. "I'll see you next week."

"Bye, Mr. Bradley," the younger boy sang in a yoo-hoo tone of voice.

"Good-bye," Conor answered, trying to remember the child's name. The other boy looked at Conor with serious eyes. He didn't utter a sound, just stared at him for a full ten seconds, then turned his attention back to the television. There was something about the older child that reminded Conor of himself at that age. It was a disturbing thought.

"Thanks for dropping these prints off, Conor." Bekka swung the door open and said good-bye over the heroic sounds coming from the television in the corner.

Striding to his truck, Conor didn't remember saying good-bye or walking the short distance from the porch to where his truck was parked. When she'd murmured his name, something deep inside him went still.

With one hand grasping his truck's door handle, he turned to take another look at the house. Its architectural style harked back to the turn of the century, when families gathered on porches to sip lemonade and watch the corn grow. A black shingled roof covered the second story. Flowers bloomed on both porches and along the curved sidewalk leading to the bricked garage. The entire effect was inviting. The house wasn't the only thing.

She'd said she was a teacher. She certainly didn't look like any of the teachers he'd ever had. But she did possess a certain air of authority teachers seemed to command. Maybe that was why his pulse rate had been completely erratic since he'd first laid eyes on her.

No, he knew better. This attraction had nothing to do with her profession. It had to do with something as elusive as tenderness, something he'd rarely had. Conor turned away and climbed into his truck. He hadn't come back to Millerton to remind himself of things he couldn't have. He came back to make an honest name for himself and to build his business.

An hour later Conor reminded himself of that goal as he punched the keys and watched the data appear on the screen before him. The tiny, cluttered office was quiet except for the occasional beep and steady hum of the computer. The noise taking place outside the room was effectively shut out by the closed door.

He rubbed his knuckles across the afternoon stubble on his chin, rechecked figures, and pressed a key. After the printer made a horrendous tapping and clattering noise, he tore the printed paper at the perforation and reached up to tack it to the cluttered bulletin board.

Outer noises of raised voices and ringing telephones suddenly invaded the quiet office. He turned as a gray-haired man entered, kicking the door shut behind him. "Have you located the shipment mix-up, Conor?"

"Here is it, Mac." Conor pointed to the board. "You'd better have one of the guys up front call the customer and explain the foul-up."

As Mac looked at the printed sheet, Conor glanced at his watch. "I've gotta go. I was supposed to be out at the new site hours ago." He stood and in three long strides reached the door. Before he'd turned the knob, the telephone rang. Conor expelled a deep breath, fighting down that old feeling of restlessness that threatened to surface.

"Jumpin' catfish! It's a madhouse around here,"

Mac muttered as he placed the receiver to his ear. "Mac here . . . Yes, he's still here . . . Yes, I'll tell him." Mac laughed at something the person on the other end of the line said, and once again Conor wondered at the other man's sense of humor.

Sitting on the edge of the desk, Mac said, "Terry needs to see you about a blueprint."

"Now?" Conor fought down that coil of pent-up energy in the pit of his stomach and turned to go.

"Conor, wait a minute."

For the people in the outer offices Conor could feel impatience. But if Mac Pearson wanted him to wait a minute, he'd wait. Without letting go of the doorknob, he stood tall, his body straight, his shoulders rigid. "Whatcha need, Mac?"

"Hell, it's not what I need, boy. It's you. Look at you. You're wound up tighter than a corkscrew. I don't think it's a good idea to push yourself so hard."

Conor stretched his neck to one side, bringing his hand up to knead the knotted muscles there. "With so much of the crew out with this flu, I have to push myself. I can handle the work load, Mac."

"It isn't just the work, boy. Something else is driving you, something besides the need to succeed. There's more to life than work, you know."

"Not where I come from, Mac."

"What about where you're going? You'll never get there if you don't learn how to relax."

Mac was in one of his Father Knows Best moods. If Conor didn't put an end to his worries in the next second or two, there was no telling where the conversation would lead. "So I'm a little wound up . . . Like I said, I can handle it, Mac. What I need is a good long run. About twenty miles might do it." One side of Conor's mouth lifted at his attempt at humor. Even he didn't run twenty miles a day.

"A long hard run, my eye! What you need is the love of a good woman."

The image of waving hair and sky blue eyes flitted through Conor's mind. This wasn't the first time he'd thought of Bekka. It had happened little more than half an hour ago when Mac's secretary had dumped the mail on Conor's desk. Having noticed Bekka's name on the price list, Annabel had said, "Mrs. Stevenson taught my granddaughter a few years back. Lovely woman. It's a shame about her husband, though. So young to be a widow, don't you think?"

Conor chased thoughts of Bekka from his mind and leaned back against the heavy door. "I'm not exactly the kind of man 'good' women are looking for, Mac."

"Maybe you just don't notice them looking. How could you when you're always working? When was the last time you came-a-callin' on a good woman?"

"Mac, I don't have time for this."

"Take the time. Since when have you become a monk?"

Conor scowled. "I'm no monk. I enjoy, ah, satisfaction, as much as the next man."

"How long since you've enjoyed any, ah, satisfaction?" Mac asked.

"What kind of question is that?" It had been a long time since he'd taken a woman to his bed. So long it shouldn't have come as such a shock the effect Bekka Stevenson had had on him.

"How long has it been, boy, since you . . ."

"I'm not going to defend my sex life to you."

Mac chuckled and sauntered to the door. "No, boy, I guess you wouldn't. It's Friday. Why don't you go out tonight? As wound up as you've been lately, it would do you good to find a woman. Hell, it would probably do you good to find two."

Conor scowled again, not bothering to voice the

string of four-letter words whirling through his head. Instead, he strode toward the front desk. Before he reached his destination, someone stopped to ask about a project and he was swallowed into the day-in and day-out chaos of Pearson Construction Company, the company he was buying into, bit by bit, the company he would help build and in turn would help him reach his goals. Mac thought he worked too hard, but Conor had worked hard all his life. This time, his work would gain him credibility.

"Imagine, whispered the townspeople. Thick, rich soup made from stones! No one will ever believe it. After all, who ever heard of stone soup?" With a soft swish, Bekka closed the book she'd read to Jimmy and Jason. Feelings of restlessness she'd been dodging since late afternoon returned. Those feelings were unusual for Bekka. During the school year Friday evenings were anticipated with longing. She spent them with Jimmy and Jason, relaxing and unwinding from the busy week of teaching. And Friday evenings during summer vacation were equally appreciated because they marked the beginning of the weekend.

Why should this Friday be any different?

"Stone soup. Ee-yuck!" Jason crowed. "I would hate to eat soup made from stones."

"But they didn't really eat the stones, sweetheart. The people of that village didn't think they had enough food to share with the soldiers. But when everyone brought just one ingredient to add to the pot of boiling stones, a delicious soup, enough to feed the entire village, was made. This book isn't really about stone soup. It's about sharing."

Jimmy was silently thoughtful, and once again Bekka wondered what her older son was thinking. She worried about her children. All parents do. But she had to worry enough for two. She had to be both mother and father to her sons. She only hoped that would be enough.

Jason, the younger of the two, was cautious in nature, but he was open about his feelings. If he was afraid, Bekka knew it. If he was angry, he let her know immediately. But Jimmy was different. Since the day he was born, he'd given her the impression that he was silently storing everything he saw and heard. Jimmy kept his feelings inside. There seemed to be a deep vulnerability within her firstborn, a hurt she couldn't heal. She wondered if this hurt had to do with memories of his father. Jimmy had been so young when Ted died. Bekka wondered how much of his father, if anything at all, he remembered.

She rose from the porch swing and wrapped her arms close to her body. Her sandals made a muted thud on the floorboards as she walked to the far side of the porch. Silent and unmoving, she looked out across her green yard to the tiny spot of garden and the fields of corn and clover beyond. For some reason her spirits were dampened. The Friday evening stretched dully into the night.

A car speeding in the distance caught her attention. Music blared from open windows as it sped down the gravel country road at daredevil speed. Jimmy and Jason heard the commotion and scurried to join their mother at the white porch railing. As the car neared their yard, it began swerving in the loose gravel. The high-pitched shrieks of laughter coming from within sent shivers down Bekka's spine.

"Who is it, Mommy?" Jason asked.

"Sounds like teenagers," Bekka replied. Didn't these kids realize how dangerous this was?

In the next instant the car did a circle spin, the churning rear wheels picking up the loose gravel and spitting it in every direction. The car's front tires barely missed the ditch on one side, the rear tires barely missed a tree on the other. Shrieks of laughter were replaced with a more terrifying sound.

From the opposite direction, an old brown truck appeared from around a slight curve in the road just beyond Bekka's property. There was little time for reaction. Bekka breathed in a rapid puff of air and held it. The truck was moving at a much slower speed, but with trees and ditches lining both sides of the road, there seemed no place for it to go. The other car came out of its spin, swerving out of control in the loose gravel. Bekka braced herself for the imminent collision, unconsciously placing a steadying hand on her sons' shoulders.

The truck lurched between two trees and over the narrow ditch in a sudden lunge for safety. The other car spun around again and again. Young people's screams, deep mouthed and loud enough to wake their echoes, raised goose bumps on Bekka's flesh.

Metal slammed against a tree, cracking like thunder in the quiet summer evening. Screaming voices became silent and the only sound was heavy-metal music blaring from the dented car's radio.

Before Bekka could form any coherent thought, she swept down the porch steps, then raced over her large front lawn. She didn't slow down until she'd nearly reached the area where the smashed car leaned awkwardly against the tree. Jimmy and Jason were behind her, advancing more slowly, watching from a safer distance.

No one appeared to be moving in the blue car, and Bekka's heart raced at what she might find. In her mind she saw another car, another accident. Pain and doubt and regrets threatened to choke her.

"Boys," she commanded, "don't come any closer."

From the corner of her eye she caught a movement.

The door of the truck opened, and as she turned, the driver's feet slid to the ground.

"Are you all right?" She uttered the words in a shaking voice as relief coursed through her, relief that was compounded as she recognized the man.

TWO

Conor planted his feet on the ground and took a deep breath. Ignoring the knot in his stomach and the ache in his temple, he strode toward the car, where steam was hissing and rising from its wrinkled hood in thin swirls. A cool hand on his arm slowed his progress, but it was the look of concern on Bekka Stevenson's face that stopped him in his tracks. Her gaze flickered to his temple where his pulse pounded like a jackhammer in his ears.

"Are you hurt?" she asked.

"I'm all right. What about them?" He motioned to the others and walked on until he reached the wrecked vehicle, wondering why her concern, her touch, made his heart ache like sore muscles after a long run.

His breath had stuck in his lungs when that car had appeared out of nowhere. His first reaction had been instinctive, and his instincts probably saved his life. He wasn't so sure the others had fared as well.

Relief coursed through him when he saw movement in the front seat of the dented car. The driver yelled for help and the passengers looked at Conor, their eyes round with shock and fear.

Conor reached inside the open window and turned the key, thereby stopping the engine and loud music. One side of the car was partially folded around a large maple tree, making it impossible to exit the vehicle from that side.

Bekka leaned down to the open window, her head near his, and peered inside. The youthful exuberance of a few minutes ago had been replaced by a stark silence. "Are you hurt?" she asked.

They all began talking at once, producing a chorus of unintelligible words. "All right, shhh everybody, it's all right." Her voice held that low, commanding quality Conor had noticed before. "If you're hurt, don't move."

The teenagers grew quiet as they slowly, jerkily unfastened their seat belts and tested their arms and legs. Satisfied that they weren't seriously injured, they shuffled out of the car. They were all able to move about, but Bekka noticed their pained expressions. One of the girls was holding her arm, another was crying. A boy had put a handkerchief to his cut forehead.

While Bekka tried to calm them, Conor ran inside to call the police and an ambulance. He replaced the phone, raked his fingers through his hair, and turned, surprised to see the two small boys standing in the doorway, silently watching.

The younger child broke the silence. "We thought you were gonna crash!"

"So did I," Conor answered. His eyes were drawn to the other child, the one named Jimmy, who stood tall, as tall as his seven-year-old body would allow. The little boy didn't utter a word, but in his eyes Conor saw such wariness. He wondered what, or who, had put it there.

Bekka turned toward the sirens wailing in the distance, growing steadily louder as they neared. They reminded her of other sirens and another accident, and for a moment icicles poked at her heart.

A police car, its lights flashing, pulled into the driveway and one of the teenagers whispered, "I'm dead. When my parents find out, I'm dead." His friends murmured their agreement.

Bekka assured them they were being overly dramatic, that their parents would be thankful they weren't seriously injured. Conor strode from the house, and her voice trailed away. Her eyes were trained on the man standing near the police car.

Conor stood straight and tall, his feet a comfortable distance apart. On anyone else, the stance would have appeared casual. Although the policeman had cut the siren, the blue and red lights continued to flash, a pulsating backdrop of color to Conor's tense features. He looked ready—ready to take on the whole world singlehandedly. Bekka wondered if she was the only person who saw the weariness, the aloneness, in his stance, in the set of his chin.

"Conor," the officer clipped.

"Vince."

"Heard you were back," the policeman said.

"Heard you became a cop."

Both men squared their shoulders and narrowed their eyes. Even from her position several feet away, Bekka could hear the sharp edge in each of their voices. She didn't understand the reason for the hostility between them. Conor and Vince had been friends as children, coming from similar backgrounds, each, in his own way, rising above them. The two men squaring off tonight weren't friends. Something had happened to the boys Conor and Vince had been, something neither of them had forgotten.

"Were you driving one of these vehicles?" Vince Macelli asked.

A muscle along Conor's jaw clenched, but all he said was "Yeah."

Behind her the volunteer ambulance team was examining the young people's cuts and bruises. Bekka walked toward the police car, not stopping until she was at right angles with the officer in blue. "Hello, Vince," she murmured. "It's nice to see you again."

"Bekka," Vince nodded. "Did you see what happened?"

She swiveled slowly, pointing to her house. "The boys and I watched the whole thing from the front porch. Those kids didn't mean any harm. I'm sure they were just out joyriding. The driver did a circle spin in the road and seemed to lose control in the gravel. Conor appeared from the opposite direction. If he hadn't gunned his engine and jumped that ditch when he did, this would have been a lot worse."

The officer walked to the road, following the skid marks in the loose gravel to the tire tracks in the grass where the truck was now parked. "You managed to jump the ditch and miss those trees?" he asked.

Conor nodded, never taking his eyes from the other man.

"How fast were you driving?"

"Thirty. A little less, maybe."

Vince Macelli asked other questions. Conor's answer to each was a slow shake of his head.

"You all right?" Vince's brown eyes seemed to delve into Conor's.

Tilting her head to one side, Bekka looked from one man's face to the other. Both men were near the six-foot mark, both dark, both proud. Something about Vince's question cut through to another level, as if they were no longer talking about the accident. At least not this one.

Conor took a deep breath, raked his fingers through his hair, and said, "I'm fine, Vince. Fine."

Vince jotted information in his notebook, took Bekka's statement, Conor's driver's license number, and his truck's license plate number, then moved on to take statements from the driver and passengers of the other car.

Curious neighbors and others who'd heard the sirens slowly drove by. Car doors slammed and voices called to one another in the gathering dusk. Parents came to get their children. Mothers cried and fathers tried not to.

Bekka accepted words of thanks from the teenagers and their parents and made small talk with neighbors and onlookers. But her gaze never strayed far from Conor. At the moment he stood in the shadows, quietly watching Officer Macelli. She followed Conor's gaze and saw Vince hand the driver of the car a ticket, then stoop to look into the boy's eyes, grasping his shoulder in an honest display of affection.

After a moment, she raised her head, her gaze searching Conor's expression, and found him looking at her. One side of his face was bathed in flashing color, casting the other side in shadow. His eyes were the darkest blue she'd ever seen, set beneath straight brows. Two lines creased his forehead, suggesting he was a man of concentration and more than an occasional scowl.

Before her stood a man who held his head high, who kept his feelings to himself. In that respect she and Conor were the same, and in that moment she felt she'd found a kindred spirit. A soft smile tipped the corners of her mouth. The smile he gave her in return was as intimate as a kiss.

There was more in the air than flashing lights, more between them than simple friendship, even though they'd never really been friends. Bekka felt carried away by her response to this man and terrified because five years ago she'd sworn she'd never be vulnerable to any man again. She was attracted to Conor, had been attracted to him when she was barely sixteen and innocent, when she'd thought she was incapable of ever hurting another human being.

His gaze traveled over her face, then dropped lower, skimming her body. She wet her lips, not even pretending to be unaffected by his look, and was rewarded with another of his devastating grins. That smile was half seduction, half playful, all male.

Vince Macelli's words, spoken nearby, broke the intimacy of the moment. "Jimmy, Jason, when are we going to talk your mom into taking the three of us to another movie?"

She felt Conor's withdrawal the moment Vince spoke. He'd reacted in a similar manner when Mara had told him her father wanted to lock Mara in the attic for dating Vince in high school.

Even though Vince and Conor had had a reputation, Bekka had never been afraid of either of them. She'd sensed then, as she did now, that their gruffness was a mask hiding their true feelings and a deep emotional pain.

Conor glanced down at the two boys, then back to Bekka before walking away. She hovered close to her children as they told Vince which movie they'd like to see, then proceeded to give him their version of the accident. Bekka smiled as the incident took on fishstory proportions as it was retold.

Vince met her smile with one of his own, straightened, closed his notebook, and slid the pen into his pocket. "How have you been, Bekka?"

"Fine, Vince. And you?" She'd dated Vince Macelli a few times last year. Even though he was fun to be with and good to the boys, Bekka didn't *feel* anything for him. Beyond friendship, that is. Until a few minutes ago, she'd wondered if she was capable of feeling anything ever again. Now she knew, and she wasn't sure she liked the answer.

Conor stood a short distance away, his hands deep in his pockets. It was pretty obvious good old Vince was interested in Bekka. Conor had no right to be jealous and no right to feel like gloating because Bekka didn't appear to return that interest.

He stayed in the background as a wrecker hauled the smashed car away, as the ambulance transported the injured teens to the hospital, and as the police car finally pulled away into the night. He examined his old pickup and found that it had escaped without a scratch. When every car, parent, neighbor, and passerby had gone, he finally breathed a sigh of relief at his near miss.

Darkness had descended on the warm June night. Crickets were chirruping in the planted fields nearby when Conor opened the door and retrieved his clipboard from the floor. Price lists and totals seemed petty and insignificant in the aftermath of police sirens and ambulances, in the aftermath of what had taken place between him and Bekka. But price lists were easier to talk about than feelings. With the clipboard tucked in the crook of one arm, he strode toward the front porch where Bekka and her sons were waiting.

He cleared his throat and gestured to the paper in his hand. "I was running the totals on the computer for the upcoming work orders. When I came to the list of materials I'll need to remodel your kitchen, I found an error."

He'd arrived back from the job site to an empty office. He'd buried his restlessness in work and, after discovering the error in Bekka's order, decided to take a leisurely drive out to the Stevenson place. The idea of seeing her house again had appealed to him, but the drive had been more stimulating than leisurely. So had seeing Bekka again.

She took the clipboard, looked at the changes he'd made, then into his eyes. They were still standing in her front yard beneath the darkened sky, and in the shadows thrown from the porch light, Conor could almost hear the warning voice whispering in her head. She had her own reasons for steering clear of involvement, reasons that had nothing to do with him. She'd given him this project, and every project would bring him closer to his goal, building Pearson Construction and making a place for himself in the town where he'd grown up. He couldn't ask her for anything more.

The boys yawned, first one and then the other. Bekka tilted her watch toward the light and extended a hand to each of her sons. "Let's go in. It's way past your bedtime."

Conor turned to go.

"Is Conor coming in, too, Mommy?" Jason asked, placing his hand in hers.

Conor regarded her quizzically for a moment, fully expecting her to send him away. "You're welcome to come inside. There's lemonade in the refrigerator, if you don't mind waiting while I tuck these two sleepyheads into bed."

He'd never been very good at waiting, but for some reason, tonight he didn't mind. He didn't mind at all.

She and the children walked ahead of him into the house, flipping on light switches along the way. Conor had walked through this very door just this afternoon. But that had been during the day and bright sunshine had shone through the tall windows. Tonight a brass lamp was lit in the corner of the room, casting soft shadows across the carpet and holding the darkness of the night at bay just beyond the windowpanes.

He followed Bekka into the kitchen, where she opened an oak-paneled door that revealed another stairway. Something deep inside him wanted to follow her up that narrow, steep staircase. Something about this woman drew him. She wasn't blatantly sexy like so many women he used to know. It was her ardent strength and inner beauty that quietly lured him nearer.

He roamed about the kitchen, imagining what it would look like when he finished remodeling it, and found himself wandering into a short hall. Before passing a darkened room, he reached inside the doorway and turned on the light. Bright yellow, blue, and red wallpaper cheered the tiny room. One wall was angled and Conor realized this room was tucked beneath that back stairway. Shelves and a large toy box were filled nearly to overflowing with children's toys.

He flipped the light switch off and continued toward the front of the house. Walking on, he came to another stairway, its oak banister reaching invitingly toward the second floor.

Above his head he heard the flat patter of small feet. In his mind, he imagined Bekka and her sons moving about in the darkened upper level. He wondered which of the rooms was hers. Had that section of the house already been remodeled? The carpenter in him aspired to view the upstairs. The maleness deep inside him longed to see the place where Bekka slept.

Conor's eyes rested on a grouping of framed photographs on one wall. A family photo with four youngsters all nearly the same size grouped tightly with their mother and father caught his attention. Two of the children were girls, and he stared at them, trying to discern Bekka from her sister. They looked so much alike, he nearly gave up until he noticed a certain spark around one little girl's eyes. That one had to be Bekka.

Then he glanced at several photographs of Jimmy and Jason. There were the usual photographs mothers kept of their smiling, round-faced babies, pouting toddlers, and handsome little boys. When he came to a picture of Bekka wearing a gray graduation gown, he stared at the blond-haired man who stood aloofly at her side, his arm draped across her shoulders. Bekka looked young, and he wondered if she'd been graduating from high school or college. The same man was photographed with Bekka and the two babies. Conor wondered if this was the man who'd put the wariness in Bekka's eyes and in Jimmy's. Whatever she'd been through, she'd tried to put it behind her. Just as he was trying to put his past behind him.

Bekka made sure the kids brushed their teeth and got into their light summery pajamas. They were too sleepy to say their prayers, and she had barely kissed each dimpled cheek good night when their even breathing could be heard and sleep came. "Pleasant dreams," she whispered to her sleeping sons.

Before returning downstairs, she pulled a brush through her tangled hair, her thoughts on the man roaming about downstairs. His deep-timbred voice had somehow reached down inside her tonight. It made her heart thud with a hollow rhythm. Maybe it was the aftereffects of the accident. Maybe it was the dark night. Whatever it was, it made her feel melancholy, blue.

Even on her tiptoes the old steps creaked in all the usual places as she hurried down the back stairway. When she didn't find Conor in the kitchen, she continued on toward the family room, where he was studying her family photographs. She crossed her arms and watched him from the doorway.

"Has anyone ever told you that everyone in your family looks alike?" he asked. His sense of humor completely surprised her. She grinned, feeling suddenly very much at ease.

"Only everyone who's ever met us." She walked farther into the room and pointed to the family photograph taken when she was a little girl. "Guess which one is me."

Without a moment's hesitation, Conor pointed to the little girl wearing the spirited smile.

"How did you know that was me?" she asked incredulously. "People can never tell Mara and me apart in that picture."

"You told me to guess. I had a fifty-fifty chance. I guess luck was on my side."

"So you're a gambling man?" This was just a game, but for some reason Bekka wanted to know more about him, more than scattered memories.

"Only when I'm pretty sure I can win," Conor replied.

She was standing close, close enough for him to smell the freshness of her hair. Close enough to be able to reach out and touch a finger to her pale cheek. Conor didn't allow the action to follow the thought. Instead he slid his hand inside his pocket and turned his attention to another photo.

Nodding toward the framed snapshot taken on her graduation day, he said, "Was this taken when you graduated from college?"

Bekka nodded and smiled in memory. "It was a race to the finish to see which would come first, my baccalaureate degree or Jimmy's birth. As you can see from the picture, I was able to graduate with my class, although Jimmy was born two days later." Together their eyes went from her graduation picture to the photograph taken two years later, the portrait of Bekka, her sons, and her husband.

"He died?"

His deep voice drew her gaze, and in answer to his question, she simply nodded.

"He doesn't look very happy."

"He wasn't."

He could have been talking about one of the babies in that picture. But they'd both known he was referring to Ted. She wouldn't have had to answer, but she'd spoken the truth. Ted hadn't been happy. He'd wanted more than she could give him, more than a wife and two beautiful children. A lifetime more, a lifetime he hadn't lived to see.

A war of emotions raged through her. The desire to explain her past to Conor fought with the need to leave it where it was. In the end, Conor was the one to make the decision. He broke eye contact and walked to the center of the room, where he bent to retrieve her price list from a low table.

"Look over this list, Bekka, and if you have any questions, give me a call tomorrow."

It was an exit line if she'd ever heard one. "Conor," she said, thinking about what he'd gone through to bring this revised list to her. He'd nearly wrecked his truck, could have lost his life.

"Hmmm?" The sound came out low and husky.

"I know it's late, but I promised you a cool glass of lemonade before you leave. Do you still want some?"

He nodded, but lemonade wasn't all he wanted. Conor wanted to touch her, to feel her smooth skin beneath his palm as he slowly ran his hand over her shoulders and down her slender arms. Touching her would have been out of the question even if she hadn't already moved away, disappearing inside the kitchen.

He followed in his own good time and watched her pour lemonade into tall glasses filled with ice cubes. She then took a fluffy kitchen towel from a drawer, held a corner under warm water, and turned to him.

"You probably didn't even know you were bleeding."

He raised his eyebrows in mild surprise. Placing two fingers to the swollen area near his temple, he gingerly touched the bump. He'd been aware of a slight throb in his temple, but he hadn't realized it had drawn blood. Actually, Conor had been more aware of the drumming of his pulse rate whenever she came near. In comparison, the ache in his temple was nondescript.

"Just as I thought," Bekka smiled. "You felt no pain."

"No brain, no pain," Conor quoted one of Mac's favorite proverbs.

"I thought that was 'No pain, no gain,' " she countered as she reached slender fingertips up to brush his hair away from the wound. Her back arched and her elbows nearly rested against his broad chest.

Conor wondered what she was thinking. Emotions he couldn't label passed through her pale gaze. He held his body perfectly still, mere inches separating them. His body reacted to her closeness; his heart pounded, his breathing deepened. He wasn't used to being touched by a woman with a smile soft enough to make him ache.

Neither said a word, and he wondered if she felt it, too, this attraction, this bond between them. It didn't take her long to complete her ministering, and before he could decide whether to kiss her or pull away, she withdrew the warm towel from his skin, and the moment was lost.

She handed him a glass and led the way to the front porch, where she lowered herself onto one side of the old-fashioned porch swing. When Conor sat at the other end, Bekka released the sigh she'd been holding. She'd been afraid he would misconstrue the intimacy of a few moments ago, and she was glad for the comfortable expanse of swing that separated them.

His dark hair had felt soft beneath her fingers. She'd gently cleaned the dried blood from his cheekbone, forcing herself to concentrate on the task rather than allow her mind to react to the sensations of feeling a man's face beneath her fingertips. She ran her thumb across her fingertips and glanced at the bump on his cheekbone. She tried to tell herself touching Conor had been no different from the countless times she'd cleaned scratches and scrapes on the boys' elbows and knees. She almost had herself convinced. Almost.

Stars twinkled in the clear sky. Insects lulled them from their hiding places in her yard and beyond. An occasional breeze ruffled new green leaves high in the trees, and the porch swing creaked ever so slightly as they slowly swayed in the quiet summer night.

Bekka chided herself for her lack of conversation. She'd invited him to stay. Why was she suddenly speechless? This man didn't intimidate her. Why, then, was she behaving like a sixteen-year-old trying desperately to think of something to say to a boy she secretly liked?

She had to say something, so she said the first thing that came to mind. "Nice night."

Conor nodded his head in agreement, then took another sip of his drink.

So much for the weather. Bekka wondered what was happening to her thought processes. Trying to think of another topic of conversation, she watched a large moth flutter dangerously near the light at the other end of the porch and was aware of Conor's every move, from the way he rested his glass on his knee to the way he pressed one foot to the floor, setting the swing in a slow swaying motion.

He slid his hand across the back of the swing, then let it fall to the seat. With hands that bore the calluses of his trade, he picked up the book she'd been reading to the boys earlier. Leafing through the brightly illustrated pages, he raised his brows. "Soup made from stones?"

"It's Jason's favorite book. I think this story's been around for at least a hundred years. Didn't your parents ever read it to you?"

She regretted the question before she'd finished asking it. It was common knowledge he'd never had the type of family life in which parents read bedtime stories to their children. When he didn't reply, she murmured, "It's never too late to read a classic."

He gave her a sidelong glance, and she was relieved to see no traces of anger or annoyance on his face. Replacing the book on the swing, he said, "I like to read. Always have." The sincerity in his voice grazed her just as surely as a touch. The tenderness in his expression moved her even more.

"Not me." At his surprise, she added, "I know what you're thinking. *A teacher who doesn't like to read?* I don't mind reading now, but I hated to when I was little. Mara's a year younger than I am, and she always had her face in a book, when she wasn't bossing the rest of us around, that is. I think I was fourteen before I read a book for the fun of it."

"She's younger, yet she bossed you?"

"The only time she admits to being younger is on her birthday, and on mine."

A sound started deep in his throat, and his laugh, when it came, was rich and warm. It changed his entire face, and she realized she'd never heard him laugh before. His eyes met hers, and his laughter faded away.

They shared a look, and for a moment there were no shadows across her heart.

She crossed her legs with a quiet swish, and Conor brought his right ankle up to rest on the knee of his left leg. She'd never been more aware of the differences between a man and a woman. Bekka didn't know just what Conor meant to her, but she was aware of an intense physical attraction and a desire to know him, the man, what he felt and what he thought, on some deeper level.

"Bekka?" His hand was large and warm, his touch on her arm her undoing. She jerked to a standing position, upsetting the gentle swaying motion of the swing.

With a scowl on his face, he followed her up. Taking his empty glass from his hand, she said, "It's getting late."

For a moment he studied her intently. "I guess it is." He expelled a long breath, and without another word he turned to leave.

"It isn't you, you know," Bekka whispered in the darkness.

He turned around slowly, first his head and then the rest of his body. "What do you mean?"

"It isn't you, Conor. It's me." Bekka watched his face, reaching into his thoughts for understanding.

An inexplicable emotion passed through his eyes. His reply, when it came, was at one with the dark night. "I think it's both of us." He smiled a small smile, and Bekka found herself doing the same, as if a weight had been lifted from her shoulders.

" 'Night, Bekka. See you next week."

She didn't move a muscle as she watched him walk down the porch steps, over the front lawn. He pulled himself up and folded his length inside his old truck. The engine rumbled to life, and he slowly pulled away onto the dirt road. She stayed where she was on the porch until his red taillights disappeared through the dust-filled darkness toward town.

She didn't know how he'd done it or why. But Conor understood. She wasn't sure what it was he understood, she wasn't sure herself. A bond had formed between them that night when she was only sixteen. She doubted he remembered it, but he hadn't forgotten it, either.

Remembering the small smile he'd given her a few moments ago made her smile. If she hadn't been feeling so lethargic, she had a feeling the reason for that smile would bother her a great deal. She went through the nightly rituals of locking doors and checking on her sons and preparing herself for bed. After allowing herself the luxury of a huge yawn, Bekka slid between her smooth sheets. She smiled into her pillow and noticed her melancholy mood had completely lifted.

_____ THREE _____

Conor parked the Chevy at the curb and cut the truck's engine, staring through the open window at the place he grew up. He wasn't sure what he'd expected to find, but he hadn't expected this. He wasn't surprised the charred rubble had been cleared away. What did surprise him was the vacant lot, the neatly mown grass. It was obvious the lot was being cared for. Why had it remained vacant all these years?

Few children were outside on this Saturday morning. He wondered how many of them were watching cartoons and tried to remember what Bekka's younger son had called his favorite cartoon.

A door slammed and children's voices called to one another down the block, and Conor realized that time had healed this neighborhood. A share of Millerton's population worked in nearby Lansing's huge auto industry. Although the future of the big automakers hadn't been secure for most of the last two decades, many of the area residents still held their jobs, building cars on the assembly line. As a result of their relative prosperity, Millerton's north end, the section formerly known as the wrong side of the tracks, had undergone a facelift.

These people were by no means rich and the houses here nowhere near as pretentious as the old dwellings on Oak Street or the newly constructed homes in the elite subdivisions on the south and west ends of town. But sagging roofs had been fixed, peeling paint replaced with new siding, and aging porches shored and painted.

Conor looked up and down the street, searching for someone, anyone, who might have known him long ago. No one appeared to have noticed his presence. Certainly no one was running him off their property. Shoving his hands deep into his pockets, he roamed to the back of the lot, where a gnarled old apple tree was still standing.

The tree had grown, but the initials carved into its trunk would never completely heal over. *C.B. #1.* Conor remembered carving those initials. He remembered the day Vince had opened his pocket knife and crossed them out, replacing Conor's initials with his own. *V.M. #1.*

Vince had been his best friend back then. His only friend. They'd always been competitors, for years managing to keep from crossing the fine line between allies and opponents. Until the night Vince had shown up, hatred flaring his nostrils, the need for vengeance severing the bond of friendship.

Vince had arrived with a split lip, and the look of disgust in his eyes had shaken Conor. For the first time, Conor had raised his fists against his friend, but he'd been no match for Vince Macelli, whose anger had made him powerful. The fist Conor had taken in his stomach had staggered him, the right hook to his jaw had knocked him cold. And all for what? For the sins of Conor's father.

Conor stared, long and hard, at the initials on that

old tree. Vince Macelli #1. In the end, it appeared that neither of them had been number one.

Conor cast another look at the vacant lot, at the bushes and vines growing wild near the back of the property. Without another glance, he turned and strode back to the curb, where he climbed into his truck and drove away.

The June morning was already warm, the fresh country air quiet except for the twittering songs of robins and sparrows. Kneeling on her pillow at the head of her sleep-rumpled bed, Bekka gazed at the summer scenery. With her elbows resting on the sill of her second-story bedroom window, she lazily watched as an approaching vehicle churned up dust in the distance.

The vibrant voice of an early morning disk jockey pulsed through the air. "It's seven thirty-one, folks, on this beautiful Monday morning . . ."

Bekka felt rested, relaxed. She'd risen early and stepped beneath the gentle spray of her shower. Donning her robe, she'd been drawn to the view outside her window. A tractor was already chugging over rich earth several fields away. Birds were chirping, the sun was shining, and in the distance a truck filled with lumber was steadily advancing.

Bekka's thought hurtled back to earth. It wasn't just any truck. It was Conor's truck.

Good grief. He's early! When he'd said he'd begin early, he'd meant early *Monday* morning. It wasn't even eight o'clock! She jumped to the floor, her bare feet scurrying over the rug on the floor at the foot of her bed. Her light robe fluttered to the rug with an airy swish. Springing to her dresser, she pulled her clothes from the drawers.

By the time she heard the tires slowly crunching over the loose gravel out front, then turn into her driveway, she was pulling loose-fitting shorts over ice blue panties. A moment later she popped her head through the rounded opening of her sleeveless shirt. Dashing past a full-length mirror, she didn't stop to look at her reflection. With one sweep of her hand, Bekka scooped up her shoes, then hurried on through the narrow hallway and down the back stairway, her bare feet slapping mutely on each stair.

Upon reaching the kitchen, she slowed her steps. Catching her breath, she combed her fingers through the waving tendrils of hair, still damp from her shower, then slid her feet into her shoes. She felt flustered and hurried. And she didn't like the feeling. Not that she would have primped for the man or anything. But she would have preferred to have had time to dress, not simply throw herself together. How professional could her damp hair possibly look?

Through the open windows she heard him cut the truck's engine, and she proceeded to remind herself that this was just another Monday. A Monday when a carpenter just happened to be coming in to begin work on her kitchen. A carpenter who just happened to be Conor Bradley.

From inside the back door, she watched as he stepped down from the cab of his old truck. Wearing laced, worn work boots, he strode over the grassy area of her side yard. The soft white material of his T-shirt stretched over his broad chest and shoulders as he lifted tools from the bed of the truck.

He obviously didn't know he was being watched. Faded blue jeans stretched over his muscled thighs. His face wore a look of concentration as he continued to unload the truck. When he bent from the waist to place a power saw on the ground, her gaze was drawn to where his jeans clung to the curve of his backside.

She slid her tongue over her dry lips and tore her

gaze away. It did absolutely nothing to put her in a more professional frame of mind. Filling her lungs with fresh air, Bekka called, "Good morning!"

The greeting brought Conor's eyes up. With one foot resting on the first step, he slowed his progress and returned the greeting.

A heavy leather tool belt dangled from one hand as he followed her into her home. A natural morning person herself, she was amazed at the way he moved, like a man with a single goal in mind. Turning to close the door, Bekka murmured, "I would offer you fresh coffee, but I'm afraid I boxed up the . . ."

He grasped an end of his tool belt in each hand, and her eyes were drawn to the flatness of his abdomen as he settled the belt more comfortably to his hips and fastened the clasp. Her nerve endings sent fluttering sensations to the surface of her skin. Those sensations seemed to meander over her body, stopping in places she thought she'd forgotten.

". . . coffee maker when I took everything out of the cupboards."

"That's okay." His words were casual enough, but the look in his eyes wasn't. He'd looked angry Friday night when he'd first stepped from his truck after the near miss with that car full of kids. He didn't look angry this morning. He looked disheartened, almost haunted.

"You're sure? I could probably find it without much trouble."

"No." He gave a resigned shrug. "Caffeine makes me tense. Believe me, I'm tense enough without it."

Tense or not, Bekka could have used a cup, a strong cup. The stronger the better. Moistening her lips, she reminded herself she had no right to be disappointed because his attitude toward her had changed and the bond they'd shared Friday night had been broken.

"Looks like you've been busy," Conor said, gesturing at the places where the refrigerator and stove had been.

"My father and brother came over last night and moved the appliances out. It's going to be interesting trying to cook on a hot plate, and I'm not really looking forward to washing dishes in the bathtub."

He leaned down to inspect the old cabinets. Opening a flimsy door, he said, "I'm afraid there's not going to be much to salvage from these old things."

"I know. Go ahead and tear them out."

"All right, today I'll take some of my frustration out on these old cupboards."

Bekka wondered about a few of his frustrations when, overhead, what sounded like half a dozen feet thumped along the upstairs floor and clunked noisily down the back stairway. The door burst open, then slammed shut. She'd never been able to understand how two such lightweights could possibly make so much noise.

"Wow, look at those saws and hammers!" Jason piped. "Mommy, can we help?"

"Boys, remember the rules. These saws and blades are dangerous," Bekka warned.

"Oh, Mommy . . ." Jason replied.

"You can watch from a safe distance. After breakfast."

"Oh, Mommy," he grumbled again.

For a moment she thought Jimmy was going to complain. For a moment she almost wished he would. But the moment passed, leaving her wondering what her older son was thinking. Like obedient ducklings, both children followed their mother from the room, watching Conor over their shoulders all the while.

Bekka dove into her morning chores with vigor. She washed the breakfast dishes in the bathroom and placed them on the cart in the living room. When she went upstairs to make the boys' beds, she found Jimmy's blankets pulled out for the second time in a matter of two days, as if he'd thrashed about in his sleep. Rather than tucking them in, she gathered the sheets from both beds. An hour later, colorful sheets and blankets billowed on the clothesline as hot, humid air pushed through, brandishing its freshness into the soft fabric.

She kept herself so busy, she shouldn't have found one single opportunity to watch Conor at work. But she did. With silent fascination she watched him plow through her old kitchen like a bulldozer charging through brush.

When the pounding in her temples began to match the pounding and crashing taking place in her kitchen, she slipped outdoors. Taking the hoe from a peg on the garage wall, she vigorously began working the garden soil.

She grasped the smooth, work-worn handle between her gloved hands and forcefully jabbed at the hard earth. With every thrust, Bekka questioned her reaction to Conor Bradley. She had openly gaped at the man, for heaven's sake! He obviously had something else on his mind and hadn't seemed to notice. What would he think of her if he had? And why did she care what he thought?

Because Conor had done nothing wrong. She'd hired him to remodel her kitchen. He hadn't come on to her, for that she was enormously relieved. She hadn't enjoyed letting men down easily these past five years, trying not to bruise their egos. She and Conor had shared a glass of lemonade and a deep look. Hadn't Bekka learned a long time ago not to place unnecessary importance on a mere look? All she and Conor had done Friday night was talk. They'd been alone together and he hadn't tried to so much as kiss her. She'd seen something in his eyes Friday night, and when he'd first looked at her this morning, before he could close his expression, she'd seen it again.

By the time she finished working the garden soil, Bekka felt better. Conor wasn't asking for anything from her, but she'd swear on a stack of bibles he needed a friend, and that's what she'd offer him. Although she doubted he remembered, it wouldn't be the first time.

Peeling the garden gloves from her warm hands, Bekka swiped the back of her hand across her damp forehead. The day was turning into a scorcher. She watched Jimmy and Jason ride their bicycles up and down the long driveway. Jimmy free wheeled, but Jason still depended on his training wheels for balance.

"Boys, don't ride too close to the road."

"We won't," Jason's voice rang through the air good-naturedly.

"We know," Jimmy called, his tone of voice reminding Bekka he thought he was too big for such reminders. She smiled to herself. She'd probably always worry.

It was well past mid-morning, and the climbing sun beat down against her exposed skin. Before heading in the direction of the garage to replace the hoe, Bekka stopped. Catching a faint breeze, she lifted her heavy hair from the back of her neck.

With a crowbar raised in mid-air, Conor caught sight of Bekka through the tall windows. For a moment, he watched her attack the garden soil with her hoe. Even in loose-fitting shorts and sleeveless shirt, she did something to his libido, and for a moment, he wished things could be different. But wishing was frustrating.

Frustration. Now that was something he understood. He also understood his body's reaction as he watched her arch her back as she lifted her hair away from her slender shoulders. He'd thought working up a sweat and tearing into her old kitchen would alleviate the tenseness in his stomach.

A new tenseness attacked his body, one that had absolutely nothing to do with work, a tenseness that had to do with the lure of a beautiful woman. It had been a mistake to go back to the old neighborhood, a mistake to relive the past.

He'd tried to tell himself Bekka's kids were the reason he couldn't pursue her. But it had nothing to do with her children. It had to do with his past, with the childhood he'd had, and the man he wanted to become. Reminding himself he had a job to do, he forced himself to return to the old kitchen. He hoped that getting his mind on the job at hand would take his mind off Bekka Stevenson's arching body. Wood cracked and nails creaked as Conor pushed the crowbar into a crevice and shoved with all his might. There was nothing like the sweat from hard physical labor to relieve frustration.

The clatter and banging of tearing wood suddenly ceased. The air seemed unusually quiet after all that racket. Walking toward the garage, Bekka caught a movement out of the corner of her eye. The side door opened and Conor began tossing pieces of old painted lumber outside. His leather tool belt rode low on his hips. The muscles in his upper arms swelled as he carried heavy pieces of the old dilapidated cupboards.

The sun's burning rays shone directly on him, and Bekka moistened her parched lips. He must surely be every bit as thirsty as she. She quickly replaced the hoe and gloves and, hurrying inside, took two tall glasses from a metal cart pushed as unobtrusively as possible by the family room doorway.

Her refrigerator looked out of place standing alone in the dining room, and she took a pitcher from inside, then filled the glasses with its contents. The sight and sound of cold lemonade pouring over crackling ice cubes reminded her of the last time she'd shared a cool drink with Conor. They'd been two acquaintances talking as they sipped lemonade on a warm summer night. This time they'd be friends.

Carrying a glass in each hand, she sipped past the ice cubes in one, the cold liquid quenching her thirst. Licking her lips, Bekka headed in the direction she'd last seen Conor. She found him near the side door, noisily throwing pieces of rubble onto a growing pile.

"Conor . . ."

With all the noise he was making, he didn't hear her. Throwing her voice into his name, she shouted, "Conor!"

Startled, he swung around, pivoting on his left leg, a stern expression tightening his face. Bekka handed the glass to him, a tentative, friendly smile on her full lips.

"You must be thirsty," she said, her way of explaining the interruption. She watched the sternness fade from his face as he slapped his hands against his jeans and reached for the tall glass.

"Now that you mention it," he agreed. The beginning of a smile stretched his mouth. Tipping the tall glass back, he practically poured the ice cold liquid down his dry throat.

Bekka watched as his chin lifted high. The long tanned column of his throat moved as he downed the entire glass of lemonade. Her fingertips were cool where they touched her icy drink, and she fleetingly wondered how the hot skin of Conor's brawny neck would feel beneath her touch. Warmth floated over her body once again, warmth that had nothing to do with friendship.

With her own glass raised to her lips, she tasted her drink. Her eyes widened over the rim as Conor lowered his chin along with the now empty glass. Looking from the glass now containing only ice to Conor's face, she slowly lowered her own glass. She'd barely taken a sip, but her thirst was completely forgotten.

Conor's darker blue gaze glided over her upturned face. His look settled on the curve of her mouth where her lips were moist with the liquid she'd been sipping. That look warmed her more thoroughly than the hot rays of the late morning sun, and she knew. He was going to kiss her.

He lowered his chin and slowly, so slowly, brought his head down to meet her upturned mouth, the shape of his head gradually blocking the sun from her view. She exhaled and her lemon-scented breath combined with his own as he touched his lips to hers, gently tasting the tartness her sweet mouth promised.

Their cool mouths joined, her lips softening in greeting. She welcomed the contact, subconsciously reacting to the feel and taste of this man. Her eyelids dropped, so that Bekka was aware only of the scent, taste, and touch of Conor. With a feather-light touch, her cool fingertips glided over his heated skin, coming to rest at the base of his throat, covering the vein pulsing there. She'd known it would be this way with him. Twelve years ago, she'd known.

Conor deepened the kiss, his mouth hungry for hers, his body hungry for more. Until her fingers had sought the skin of his neck, their only point of contact had been their mouths, touching and tasting. When she'd touched him, heat sliced through his body, and he reacted, instantly, in a totally masculine way.

His glass was held in one hand, the ice within melting fast from the heat of his hand and from the warmth of the sun. He pressed his other hand to the smooth blade of her shoulder, gently sliding his large palm over her back. The gliding pressure brought her closer until her body rested completely against him. His heart hammered in his chest, and she felt so incredibly soft, nestled against his hard body.

She made a sound deep in her throat, and Conor answered with a sound of his own. This reaction from Bekka was more than he'd anticipated, more than he could have asked for in his wildest dreams. His lips had touched hers and all thoughts fled his mind. For this moment, only the sensations of Bekka remained; her warm mouth moving against his, her breath mingling with his own, her soft body pressed tightly to his.

Snickering.

From somewhere far away, she heard the sound of children's giggles and loud whispering. Bekka became aware of the buckle on Conor's tool belt pressing into her waist, and with that awareness, she realized the snickered giggles were coming from nearby.

Her emotions skidded to a stop as the shock of what she'd just felt hit her full force. Stepping back, she took a quick breath. Conor's hand fell away from her back to rest idly at his side, yet the warm imprint of his work-roughened palm lingered along her skin.

Her gaze darted to her children who stood, giggling, a few feet away, then flickered back to Conor. She felt the blush on her cheeks but could do nothing but stand there, in the bright mid-day sunshine, tongue-tied. Being caught by her own children, kissing a man, was a new experience.

"Whatcha doin', Mommy?" Jason asked.

"They were kissin', you dummy," Jimmy answered.

"I know they were kissin'," Jason rolled his eyes expressively. "Why were you kissing Conor, Mommy?"

Bekka settled her free hand to her hip and struggled to find an explanation. She didn't know why she'd kissed him. She only knew she'd always wanted to.

"When grown-ups like each other, they sometimes kiss," Conor replied, saving Bekka from struggling with another answer. She heard the deep tremor in his voice and knew that he, too, had been touched by that kiss.

She was aware their kiss had to do with liking. She also knew it went beyond simple liking. It had to do with wanting. Bekka had wanted before, deeply, completely. It had left her vulnerable. A long time ago she'd learned that being vulnerable led to pain.

"Conor?" Jason asked. "Can me and Jimmy help you throw this old wood onto that pile?"

Conor's eyes darkened in the bright sunlight as they met Bekka's in an unspoken question. Her gaze slid from his magnetic gaze to her sons. "Go ahead, boys," she said. "While you help Conor, I'll fix lunch."

She took the tall glass from Conor's hand, being careful not to touch him in the process. Jason and Jimmy climbed the steps, ready to help, suddenly feeling very important, the scene they had just witnessed between Conor and their mother seemingly shrugged aside.

The boys chatted while they threw old lumber onto the pile, and the knife Bekka held as she spread tuna on bread clinked to the table. She listened to Conor's deep voice, which echoed as much as the boards bouncing like thunder on the growing pile. The sound reached her ears through the open window, and she flattened her palms against the cool tabletop.

Just hearing Conor's voice brought the memory of the firm touch and musky scent of him to Bekka's mind. She was proud of the life she'd built for herself and her children. She'd managed to put the past behind her, and her plans for the future were clear. Those plans didn't include kissing Conor Bradley, nor did they include wanting to kiss him again. She'd thought the part of herself that reacted to a man's touch was dead, frozen for eternity.

Until now.

Conor Bradley was uncharted territory. When he was near, a part of her former personality, a part she thought she'd left behind, resurfaced. It was her spontaneity that had brought her and Ted together, and that one romance had been the base for all the pain she'd experienced in her adult life. When he died, she'd sworn off romance. Permanently.

The problem was, Conor made her feel romantic. His look, his deep-timbred voice, his touch. Bekka closed her eyes as she fought against those romantic notions. It may be a struggle, but Bekka had learned to live with struggle.

Ignore his attraction. suppress your awareness. At least until he finishes the kitchen. That's what she would do. Her mind was willing, but her body couldn't seem to forget that long, tender kiss.

She was strong. She had somehow gotten through Ted's funeral. She'd been forced to accept people's sympathy and well-meant intentions knowing what she knew about her husband. And she hadn't crumbled. If she could get through that sad, bleak time, Bekka was absolutely certain she could control her emotions for a few short weeks, until Conor finished the kitchen. Armed with her new sense of objectivity and confidence, she went to call the boys in for lunch.

Bekka stood inside the screen door, absorbing what appeared to be the peaceful atmosphere Conor and her sons shared. Birds tweeted somewhere high in the branches of green leafy trees. A neighbor's tractor labored with a low rumble in a field far across the section.

Conor was resting on the warped floorboards of the old porch. Leaning against the railing, he dangled one foot off the edge, letting it swing in a half-circle. The other he pulled up closer to his body, resting one arm on his bent knee. From all outward appearances, he looked perfectly calm. His clenched jaw and the vein pulsing at his throat were at odds with his casual facade. He had something on his mind, something serious.

Jimmy and Jason were perched on the steps, their young faces bright from the exertion of their labors. Bekka's older son seemed to have shed the wariness he normally reserved for new acquaintances.

"Jason . . . Jimmy . . . Lunch is ready." The boys jumped up, their feet moving before they hit the floor, their stampeding footsteps echoing on the hollow boards. "Wash your hands and I'll be there in a minute."

Conor pushed himself off the porch, brushing bits of rubble from his worn jeans. Standing on the ground, he looked up at her face.

"We're having tuna sandwiches and you're welcome to join us for lunch."

"No, thanks," he refused politely. "I'll catch a bite to eat in town. I should be back out here in about an hour." Something had been nagging at him all weekend, something about that lot, something about the initials carved in that apple tree. Something didn't add up.

"Pardon me?" she asked.

He hadn't realized he'd mumbled his thoughts out loud. He looked into her eyes, his gaze lingering there for a moment. "Never mind. I'll see you in an hour."

He unhooked the buckle of his tool belt and tossed it inside the cab of the old truck. Without glancing her way, he hoisted his foot onto the running board, the washed-out material of his jeans stretching over his thighs, reminding him how Bekka's thighs had felt pressed to his. The memory of that kiss was potent. His body still strummed with desire, and he knew it would take a long run later that evening to tire his body enough to make him forget.

He turned the key and ground the lever into reverse, then made the mistake of looking at her face. Understanding softened her gaze, and a vague memory bounced along the edges of his mind. He'd seen that smile before. It haunted him, as much as the initials carved in that old apple tree.

FOUR

Conor crushed the paper sack containing the remains of his fast-food lunch and hurled it into a trash can nearby. He'd consumed the food with little enjoyment, seated in the overheated cab of his truck. The windows were down, but the hot noon sun punished the sweltering pavement, the oppressive heat rising in waves.

Two things he was trying not to think about scrambled through his mind—Bekka's kiss and that vacant lot. One had nothing to do with the other, but both had taken root in his subconscious.

He took a deep breath, jerked the shifting lever into reverse, and backed out of his parking space. Slamming the lever into first, he pulled into traffic, checked his rearview mirror, and, out of the blue, turned left at the first intersection.

The warm air streaming in through the open windows did little to bring relief to his prickly skin, but the heat was the least of his concerns. Conor pulled up to the curb and cut the engine, his gaze following the boy pushing the lawn mower across the narrow lot. He'd had no intention of coming back here. Now that he had, he couldn't bring himself to leave.

An older man who'd been watching the boy's progress from the shade next door stood and ambled toward him. Conor found himself walking around the front of the truck. With hands on his hips, he met his former neighbor halfway.

"Conor Bradley. Thought I saw this truck parked out here the other day. I always knew you'd come back."

"How have you been, Bud?" Conor couldn't remember a time when kids in this neighborhood had called adults mister or miss. Friendly or not, they'd grown up on a first-name basis.

Bud Trierweller smiled a somewhat sheepish, bucktoothed grin as he said, "Not bad, boy. Ain't complainin'." Turning his head, he added, "Place looks good, don't it?"

Conor nodded.

"Just wanted to thank you." The older man's eyes darted nervously from Conor to the boy mowing the grass.

Old man Trierweller wanted to thank him? The same man who'd run him off his property with a broom when he was twelve was thanking him now?

"The money Loretta and I got for keeping this place up really came in handy over the years. You're sure you're happy with the job we've done?"

For a long moment Conor stared at the older man, trying to comprehend what Bud's question had to do with him.

"You plannin' on building, now that you're back and all? I know it ain't none of my business, but Loretta and I have the boy here, what with our Dolores getting divorced and all, and I was just wonderin' what you were planning to do, because this here job's good for a youngster."

Conor only half listened as he struggled with Bud's

implications. For some reason the other man was under the impression that this property belonged to Conor.

"Are you gonna take over the upkeep, now that you're back?"

Conor remained perfectly motionless for a moment, not certain his mind and body were functioning together. When he finally met Bud's gaze, he said, "I'm not planning to make any changes right now, Bud."

The other man grinned again. Grasping Conor's hand, he shook it profusely. "Good. And just so you know, I never believed you set that fire. Never could figure out why Leroy Macelli claimed you did. Oh, I know I wasn't too nice to ya back then. I blame that on the bottle. Haven't had a drop in over eight years. Just wanted you to know your lot's in good hands."

Conor thanked his old neighbor, not conscious he'd drawn his brows downward, deep in thought. He hadn't known Vince's father had started a rumor like that, but he wasn't surprised he had. What he'd never understood was the man's hatred for him. Conor had never known what he'd done to warrant such an emotion.

Conor said good-bye to Bud and sauntered back to the truck. Before letting out the clutch, he cast one last look at the freshly mown grass, the gray-haired man waving from the sidewalk, and the old apple tree near the back of the lot. He pushed the lever into first gear and rounded a corner, heading toward the country. Questions bombarded him, questions he'd asked himself a million times, and questions Conor had never considered before.

"Bek . . . turn your TV on . . . I can't believe I'm running this late. I'm missing the wedding." As always, Mara infected the air around her with a medley of jumbled confusion.

She'd burst through the front door, her toddling son

Marc on one hip, a diaper bag strapped to one shoulder, two blond-haired little girls skipping ahead of her. "We waited forever at the pediatrician's office and now I'm missing Rand and Audrey's wedding."

Shaking her head, Bekka leaned down to turn the TV set on. Mara claimed she lived for her soap opera. Maybe that was why she was an eternal matchmaker.

The TV burst on the same instant Jimmy and Jason joined the mayhem, and Mara's twins, Mindy and Missy, shrieked as they zigzagged between furniture and people, chasing their cousins. The four children were masters at this game.

Bekka reached for baby Marc as Mara grabbed her daughters' hands. "Shh! Look, girls. We're not too late. Doesn't Audrey look beautiful in her wedding gown?"

All five children were suddenly quiet as they watched the wedding scene taking place on the TV screen. When Rand lifted Audrey's veil and lowered his head for the dramatic kiss, Jason turned beguiling eyes to his Aunt Mara and said, "They kiss just like Conor and Mommy!"

Bekka's cheeks warmed in remembrance. She'd hoped Jason had forgotten that kiss. Unfortunately, he hadn't. Neither had she. Her embarrassment turned to annoyance as she met Mara's knowing look, but before she'd said a word, her gaze was drawn to her firstborn.

Jimmy regarded her with somber curiosity. The girls were talking about Audrey's gown, but Jimmy held her look. Once again she wondered what her young son was thinking behind those watchful blue eyes. She wanted to ask, to grasp his narrow shoulders and demand that he tell her what was wrong. Mindy and Missy giggled, continuing in their noisy pursuit of their boy cousins, and the moment was lost.

"If you're going to run, go outdoors!" Mara commanded. Little Marc chose that instant to try to wriggle out of Bekka's arms, and the door slammed as the older children ran outside. After leaning down to set Marc free, Bekka looked at her sister, who was completely ignoring the wedding scene.

"For someone who couldn't take the time to drive home lest she'd miss this program, you aren't paying very close attention, Mar."

In the background the high-pitched voices of their children and the steady rap, rap, rap of a hammer could be heard. Bekka peeked out the window, her eyes following the kids' progress across the side lawn. When she turned back, she pretended interest in the soap opera on TV. With a lightning-fast motion, Mara flicked the television off, and Bekka ran out of diversions.

"You kissed him?"

Pride kept Bekka from cowering beneath Mara's know-it-all attitude. "You're always telling me I should pay closer attention to the opposite sex."

"The opposite sex. Not Conor Bradley!"

"As far as I can tell, Conor's a member of the opposite sex." Bekka smiled to herself at that understatement, and the baby toddled away toward the noises in the kitchen. Mara harrumphed and followed her son. Bekka decided to do the same.

Through the new windows on the kitchen's west wall, Conor's form was silhouetted against the backdrop of bright sunshine. Sweat glistened over the rippling muscles of his arms as, oblivious to their watchful gazes, he effortlessly lifted heavy boards and two-by-fours.

"You actually kissed Conor Bradley?"

"Mara, he doesn't have the plague. You dated Vince years ago, so you should know neither of them was really bad. They never did anything seriously wrong, except be born into families that couldn't care for them the way ours did for us.''

By the time Bekka had finished, Mara's arched brows had smoothed. After a brief silence, she said, ''So, how was it?''

Bekka shook her head. ''None of your business.''

''Oh, Bekky, don't be so defensive. I'm no snob, and I know Conor never got into real trouble. But do you really believe he's the man for you?''

Bekka shot her a warning look, and Mara held her hands up in defeat. ''Just tell me this. Are you planning to kiss him again?''

''I don't have to answer that, you know. But for your information, no, I'm not planning to kiss him again. It was just one of those things that happen sometimes. And for the record, I don't think he's planning a repeat, either.''

It was true. Conor had arrived back from lunch early, but kissing her seemed to be the last thing on his mind. He'd said little, going about his work with single-minded determination. He did the work of two men, hadn't taken a break, hadn't met her look. As a result, her old cabinets were completely torn out, the old molding pulled off. At this rate, he'd finish with the job in record time.

''What are you going to do?'' Mara asked in a voice of authority as she followed Bekka to the refrigerator in the dining room.

''He's working up a sweat out there in the hot sun. I'm filling glasses with sun tea and then I'm going to offer him something cool to drink. You can have something, too, or . . .'' She let the words trail away.

''The last time you were this determined to go against my advice was when you decided to marry Ted.''

The words rang hollow in the air. They'd hit their

mark, and Bekka could think of nothing to say in her defense.

"I only hope you know what you're doing." Mara picked up her baby and headed toward the side door. As if she regretted her harsh words, she took a deep breath and turned back to Bekka, offering her an apologetic smile. "As long as you aren't planning on becoming involved with him, there's no reason we should let him die of thirst."

"My point exactly." Bekka turned back to her task and poured the remaining tea into the tall glasses, remembering the last time she'd taken Conor something to drink. She wondered how long it would take to forget the taste of lemonade on his warm lips. She closed her eyes against the invading memory, picked up the tray, and hurried out the door.

Conor welcomed the idea of a cool drink, and his eyes feasted on the sight of Bekka. She moved easily down the steps, a tray of sparkling drinks in her steady hands. Her hair fell across her shoulders, sunshine weaving the waving strands with gold. Leaning over, she placed the tray on the tailgate of his truck, and Conor caught a glimpse of a narrow strap. He tore his gaze away and chided himself for looking in the first place. He'd have thought it would take more than the mere sight of a bra strap to trip his libido.

"Conor, would you care for a glass of iced tea?" Mara asked, not even trying to hide her censure. Bekka looked as if she wanted to nudge her sister, and Conor wondered if they'd just had an argument. He accepted the glass and took a thirst-quenching swallow.

"So, Conor, Jason tells me you've been kissing my sister."

Tea splashed down his throat, catching halfway. He

choked, then gasped for air. Bekka gasped for an entirely different reason. "Mara!"

Mara, not looking the least bit contrite, said, "I know how to get a conversation rolling, don't I?"

"One of these days, Mar, you're going to get yours," Bekka warned.

"What have I done?" Mara asked sweetly.

While Bekka recounted a few of Mara's latest schemes, Conor swiped the back of his hand across his mouth and studied the two sisters. As before, they looked incredibly alike. But there were also differences, some subtle, some not. Mara wore her hair in a shorter style, and she was in a constant flurry of motion. In comparison, Bekka seemed like a beacon of calm. That calm drew him like cool shade on a hot day.

"No, no, Marc. Ladybugs aren't for eating," Mara crowed, flicking the little bug from her son's fingers.

The child was getting cranky from the constant, though necessary, supervision of his mother. Mara took a large gulp of her tea, then picked up her active baby, saying, "Okay, Tiger, let's call your sisters and we'll all go home so you can take a nice long nap." Without taking a breath, she raised her voice and called to her daughters. "Missy, Mindy! It's time to go."

Conor's head was momentarily turned away from Mara, but he didn't miss the shrug she gave Bekka. Nor did he miss the stern look Bekka returned. He watched from a distance as Mara said something to her sister, and he almost smiled as Bekka answered, sliding her hand behind her back to hide her crossed fingers.

His gaze moved slowly over her, and he imagined kissing those crossed fingers, imagined kissing her wrist and moving upward to the soft skin of her shoulders. His body drew tight as he imagined her kissing him in return. Those thoughts stirred desire deep in his body.

He could understand if desire was all he felt, but his feelings went beyond simple desire.

With a honk and the same flurry of activity with which they'd arrived, Mara and her brood drove away. With his back to Bekka, he looked out across the fields bordering her yard and asked, "Do you two argue often?"

Bekka hadn't known he was even aware of her presence. As casually as she could manage, she said, "Only when she butts into my life."

"You handle her."

For a moment she studied him intently, then a smile settled to her lips. "I do, don't I?"

He turned to face her, and his silent nod and subtle smile stole over her. His manner soothed and drew her. He finished the rest of his drink and turned back to the pile of lumber on his truck, talking as he worked. "What did she call her children?"

"Missy, Mindy, and Marc."

"Mara, Missy, Mindy, and Marc? What's her husband's name?" he asked, sliding a two-by-four from the stack.

"Mike Miller."

He swung another board off the truck and dropped it to the ground. "Mike, Mara, Missy, Mindy, and Marc Miller?" Conor laughed. He actually laughed, and the heady, melodious sound circled an empty space in her heart.

Her eyes roamed over his face, and she saw her desire mirrored in his eyes. In reaction to his sensuous look, her voice lowered perceptibly. "If you knew the rest of my family, you'd understand."

"There's more?"

"My parents' names are Frank and Emma. Having gone through life with such common names, they decided to give their children unusual names. Thus, Todd,

Bekka, Mara, and Dustin. You already know Mara's family's names. Todd married his high school sweetheart, Tammy, and they're expecting their first child in October. You'll never guess what they want to name that child is it's a boy.''

"What's your maiden name?" He dropped a heavy board and stared into her eyes.

"Taylor."

"Todd and Tammy Taylor?"

Bekka laughed. His humor was an unexpected gift. "Tyler."

"Todd, Tammy, and Tyler Taylor? Maybe they'll have a girl."

She shook her head. "Todd says if the baby's a girl, he wants to name her Taylor. Taylor Taylor. My father shakes his head whenever anyone mentions these crazy names. He says talking about his grandchildren makes him stutter."

"So, Jimmy's and Jason's names aren't a mere coincidence?"

"Yes and no. Their father's name was Ted, which didn't exactly go with Bekka. When Jimmy was born, he didn't care what we named him, so I chose my grandfather's name. Then, when Jason came along a year later, I chose another name beginning with *j*. I guess in my family it's becoming a tradition."

He met her smile with one of his own, but beneath his grin, Bekka sensed a shadow, a jagged vulnerability. It was deeply buried, nearly hidden to the rest of the world. But not to her. That touch of sensitivity, no matter how disguised, added to the current of awareness between them. She rolled her cool glass across her forehead, as much to cool her body as to cool her thoughts.

Conor took a navy handkerchief from a hip pocket and wiped a film of sweat from his brow. He couldn't remember the last time anyone had looked at him this way, with a glint of wonder, as if she'd discovered something special, something as fleeting as summer lightning.

He followed the trail of Bekka's glass as she rolled it across her forehead, and he wanted to press his lips to her cool skin. With one arm resting on a step behind her and the other raised to her forehead, her back was arched, and her breasts drew his attention. He fought the impulse to cover them with his fingers, to measure their weight in the palm of his hand. That wanting spread through his body in a wave of heat that had nothing to do with the afternoon sun.

She had the power to make his body throb, his mind forget, without doing anything, by simply being near. He wondered what she'd do if he touched her, wondered what she'd say if he took her to see his old neighborhood, if he showed her the initials carved in that old apple tree.

"Conor."

His brows flickered, his gaze gradually focusing on Bekka. She'd leaned ahead and was looking deep into his eyes. She'd touched his arm, was touching him still.

His gaze clung to hers, then shifted to the stack of wood at his feet. He had a job to do, a mystery to unravel. And nothing to offer a woman like Bekka. He knew it, her sister knew it. He wondered if Bekka knew it, too.

He stood, brushing his hands on his jeans, and said, "The weather man predicted this scorcher today." He didn't look at her but knew she'd risen, too.

"They're calling for this heat wave to last through the weekend," he added. He still didn't look into her eyes, didn't want to see her disappointment. She picked up his glass and slowly walked inside, and once again Conor felt he'd lost something precious, something he never knew he'd had.

* * *

The following morning Conor strummed his fingers on the steering wheel in agitation and clenched his jaw, impatiently staring from his watch to the dark window of the city office. A light finally came on at two minutes past eight, and his agitation grew as he saw two middle-aged women talking, slowly pouring coffee. "Come on, people. Not everyone has all the time in the world," he sputtered under his breath. "Unlock the frigging door."

Exactly three minutes later, one of the women turned the lock. Conor sprang from the truck and strode inside, startling the woman at the door. "Mercy!" she exclaimed, her hand flying to her throat.

He had the presence of mind to apologize, and the woman said, "Can I help you?"

"I'm Conor Bradley and I'd like to see your tax roll for Five-Thirteen North Maple."

She pulled a large black book from beneath a shelf and began leafing through the pages. Conor tried to tamp down his impatience at her turtle speed. Finally, she pointed to the property description and Conor peered at the tax-roll number. Bud Trierweller was right. The property was in his name. How could that be?

He'd assumed the property had been sold years ago at a tax sale. Apparently that wasn't the case. Who'd been paying the taxes all these years? And why was the property in his name?

Those questions weighed on his mind as he muttered a quick thank you and turned to leave. The woman's high-pitched voice slowed his progress. "Mr. Bradley, what's your address?"

"My address?"

"Yes," she said, fumbling through her drawer. "Now that you're here, I'll have an address so I can return your receipts. I've saved them all these years. I know they're here somewhere.'' She held up an envelope triumphantly. ''Here they are. You were taking quite a chance sending all that cash through the mail each year. But not to worry, I'm as honest as the day is long.''

Her words thrummed through his brain. Conor accepted the envelope, turned on his heel, and abruptly left the building. ''Mr. Bradley, your ad—'' The door closed on her remaining words.

He started the truck and riffled through the tax receipts in the long envelope. Every one had been paid. By whom? The gears ground as he pulled away from the office and the word *whom* ground through his mind. Only one person came to mind.

Minutes later he strode through another parking lot and circled to the rear of another building. He entered through a seldom used door and took the steps two at a time. Pushing through a heavy wood door, he threw all twelve receipts onto the cluttered desk.

''Holybejesus, Conor! You tryin' to give me a heart attack?'' Mac shot at him with a rare scowl. Taking the envelope in his hand, he continued. ''What are these?''

''I was hoping you could tell me.''

The older man took all twelve tax receipts from the envelope. After leafing through them, he met Conor's look. For once, Mac didn't spout some trite saying.

''Well?''

Mac's voice was as composed as his actions when he finally said, ''Tax receipts for Five-Thirteen North Maple. That's in your old neighborhood, isn't it?''

''Go on.''

''What do you mean *go on*?'' Mac's voice was too emotional, his expression too surprised to be dishonest.

''You mean you don't know anything about these receipts?''

"Why would you think I'd know something about them? What's going on, Conor?" Mac's eyes were sharp and assessing.

"You didn't pay these taxes, Mac?" Conor needed to hear him say it.

"Leapin' lizards, boy! I don't know what you're talking about, but no, I didn't pay these taxes."

Conor sank into a chair. With hands on knees, he narrowed his eyes as Mac looked through all the receipts. "Why would I pay *your* taxes? Besides, I've been here only six years. These date back twelve."

Running his hands through his hair, Conor tried to explain. "I don't know what's going on, Mac. I went out to the old place yesterday. Old man Trierweller thanked me for paying him to keep the yard up. He thanked *me*. So this morning I went to the city offices to take a look at the tax description. The place is in *my name*. I haven't paid those taxes, and my old man died the year after we left. If it wasn't you, who did it?"

Mac's chair squeaked as he leaned back. "I don't know, boy. But you're barking up the wrong tree."

Conor studied the man sitting behind the desk. Mac Pearson was the father he'd wished he'd had, a friend, and a respected business partner. Mac had seen a young boy's potential, claimed he'd had a feeling that the proud hooligan would turn out to be the best carpenter he'd ever hired, and told anyone willing to listen he was glad he'd followed his instincts.

They'd met on a rainy October day over eleven years ago. Conor had driven his old Malibu past a huge brick house in the throes of remodeling. He'd parked his car and stood looking at the crew unloading a truck in the rain. A gray-haired man the crew called Mac was overseeing the work. When an argument between two lazy laborers turned into a fistfight, Mac broke it up and fired them on the spot. He'd watched the men saunter away and met Conor's gaze. Sizing him up, Mac had said, "You lookin' for work, boy?"

Conor didn't remember answering, but moments later he'd found himself with his first rewarding job. That first project had changed the course of his life. He was a fast learner, an avid apprentice. He'd taken architectural courses at night and worked with Mac in Detroit for five years. Six years ago Mac and his wife decided to move to Millerton, a relatively small city a hundred miles to the northwest. Even though it was the town where Conor had grown up, he had no real ties to Millerton and had stayed with the old company.

They'd kept in touch, Mac being the closest thing Conor had to family. Then, six months ago Mac told him there was something important he wanted to discuss. Mac said the business was getting too big for one man and offered Conor a junior partnership.

Conor had driven through the streets of Millerton, past the dime store where he'd bought red licorice, past the used car dealer where he'd bought his first car, and was surprised to learn that all his memories weren't bad.

Mac was the only person he'd told about his past, about his father and the fire that had nearly claimed both their lives. He'd owed Mac a great deal, but that wasn't the reason Conor had accepted the offer. He had no doubts Mac could have found another partner. Conor had accepted the job out of pride, and he wasn't sorry he had. He'd sold his house, given notice at his other job, and arrived back in town less than two months ago.

"Any idea who paid these taxes, boy?" Mac's words brought him to the present.

"Not a clue." But there was another person, another man's image, cutting into Conor's mind.

He stood, grasped the envelope of receipts, and

strode to the door. "I'd better be going, Mac. Bekka will wonder where I've been."

"Bekka, hm?"

"Yeah, Bekka."

"You're on a first-name basis with the Stevenson woman?" Mac asked with a smug grin.

"This time you're the one barking up the wrong tree, Mac."

Mac's bout with speechlessness was over. "You're as fidgety as a cat in a sack, Conor ole boy, and I'd be willing to bet the Stevenson woman has something to do with it."

"Forget it, Mac."

"Bring her around some night next week. Betty would love to meet her." Conor didn't answer, and Mac's deep chuckle followed him out the door.

Bekka and Conor had established a routine. As on the three previous mornings, she presented Conor with a cool glass filled with iced tea, lemonade, or cola, and together they took a short break on her back porch. She hadn't touched him since the day she'd rested her hand on his arm, since the day he'd straightened, changing the subject to the weather. She hadn't delved into any deep conversation, nor had she looked deep into his eyes.

She was warm and friendly. Nothing more, nothing less, and Conor found himself yearning for something unattainable. He wiped his brow with the back of his hand and accepted the glass, again noting her care not to touch him.

Jason came into view, pedaling his bike around the wide turn before he headed back down the length of the driveway. His red shorts and T-shirt made a colorful splash against the country background. Conor had finally found a sure way to tell the boys apart. They looked incredibly alike, both blond, both blue eyed. But Jimmy, the older boy, had wavy hair, and Jason's was bone straight.

That straight hair of his didn't even bend in the wind. It blew straight back as Jason vigorously pumped his legs up and down as he pedaled. "He doesn't even use those training wheels except when he turns."

"I know, but just try to talk him out of them. Jimmy calls him a scaredy cat, but I prefer to think of him as cautious."

Like his mother, Conor thought to himself. To Bekka, he said, "Which of the boys is more like you?"

"It's hard to say. Jason is more open. My mother says I was like that at his age. But she can tell horror stories about the scrapes I got myself into when I was small. And Jason isn't like that at all. Jimmy is the one to think up mischief. He's more like I was in that respect, only Jimmy keeps so much inside."

Conor thought the older child was more like Bekka than she realized. The Bekka who sat on the porch step sipping lemonade was talkative and congenial. But there was a part of her she kept locked away. Gone was the glow in her eyes. Gone, too, was the woman who had kissed him so completely.

"You got into scrapes when you were a child? I find that hard to believe."

"Well, believe it. Sometime when my brothers or Mara come over to check up on me, ask them about our childhood."

The fact that she didn't appreciate her family's interference was evident in her voice. Much of what she was feeling came through in the directness, the softness, and the sultriness of her voice. For a moment, he thought he could listen to her voice forever, and *forever* was a word Conor seldom contemplated.

"Jason is cautious by nature. I had to learn to be cautious the hard way."

"Yeah?" he asked. "I think I was born cautious."

For the first time in three days, Bekka looked, really looked, into his eyes. A heaviness had centered in her chest when Conor had rejected her touch and her offer of deeper friendship, aching like an old wound on a rainy day. He didn't want her friendship. Why should she agonize over it?

Something was driving Conor, but she knew in her heart something was driving her, too. They both carried too much old baggage, too must pride and past pain. A relationship would be disastrous. Knowing that didn't keep the yearning from her heart, didn't keep her thoughts from returning to their kiss.

She broke eye contact and stood. "Break's over," she declared, then stood slightly back and watched him work.

The boards he carried into the house hit the floor with a loud thud. Conor bent his knees, squatting down to mark an exact measure with a square carpenter's pencil. A wan shaft of sunlight touched his dark hair. She'd perceived him as tough and resilient, but from this angle, he seemed in need of a soft touch, a gentle smile.

She remembered the way his hair had felt beneath her fingers the night of the accident in her front yard, when she'd smoothed his hair away from his skin. Bekka fought the urge to comb her fingers through his hair again. Instead, she curled them into her palms, her eyes scanning the area where the bump had been. All that remained was a faint bruise beneath the tan of his skin. He must be a fast healer. Tough and resilient was probably pretty accurate.

Conor pressed a button and the tape measure glided neatly inside its metal case, and it occurred to her she knew very little about him. She'd overheard the older girls' giggles and claims that their knees turned to putty if he so much as looked their way. She knew he'd become a fine carpenter, but that was all. For reasons she didn't want to dwell on, she wanted to know more. "Where are you living, Conor?" she asked.

"Where?" he repeated.

"I mean, where's home?"

He cocked his head to one side and leveled his gaze at her. "I'm renting a place over on East Lowell, but it isn't really home. I just found out the old lot's in my name, but that never was much of a home."

"Why wouldn't the old lot be in your name? If you didn't sell it . . ."

"I was just a kid when I left, Bekka. And my old man died a year later. I didn't intend to come back here, and I assumed the place would have been sold for back taxes. But it wasn't."

"Why wasn't it?"

"Good question. The taxes are paid up."

"By whom?"

"I don't know."

By the look in his eye, Bekka thought he had at least a vague idea. "Do you have any family near here?" she asked gently, because she sensed a loneliness deep within him, one he didn't mention but couldn't quite hide.

With that question he straightened, settling one hip against the sawhorse. "My mother took off right after I was born, and there wasn't much family."

She didn't utter any of the inadequate, superficial words people used at times like these. He didn't seem to want sympathy for something that had happened years ago, and she didn't offer any.

"Is your mother still living?"

Conor stared into her light blue eyes, crossed his

arms over his chest, and said, "As far as I know, she died when I was a child."

"You're sure?"

"It isn't something I'd lie about."

Laying her hand on his arm, she said, "Oh, Conor, I'm not sure whether it's the teacher in me or the mother in me, or maybe Mara is rubbing off. I didn't mean to insinuate you'd lie. I'm just trying to help you come up with a plausible explanation."

Her hand warmed his arm, her voice warmed his soul, but it was her smile that heated his heart. He'd never known a woman like Bekka, a woman with a smile soft enough to penetrate his tough skin.

She'd known she was going to touch him before she felt the coarse hair spring beneath her palm. Her gaze rested on her hand where it rested against the deeper shade of his skin. Her heart rate accelerated, and she was aware that the feelings he had aroused in her days ago still simmered deep inside her.

Bekka sensed his loneliness, and somewhere deep in her soul she wanted to fill just one of his empty spaces. But she had learned the painful lesson that people can't fill other people's emptiness. She'd tried with Ted. And she'd failed. Miserably.

She saw the battles taking place behind his eyes, and a part of her exulted because she knew he felt it, too, this unnameable emotion lurking between them. Progress on the kitchen was coming along nicely. But progress with reaching this man was coming much more slowly. He needed her. Whether he knew it or not. What frightened her was that she might need him, too.

She quickly removed her hand from his arm. Just as quickly, he resumed measuring.

"What are you going to do?" At his compelling look, she added, "About that lot. What are you going to do with your lot?"

"I don't know," he returned, and she thought he was going to leave it at that until he added, "It doesn't feel like mine. It never did." He'd spoken the words with a shadow of remorse and she understood how alone he really was.

When she remembered the one time she'd come face to face with him in her youth, she remembered him as a hero, as a young boy bearing a black eye, the battle scar of a fight he'd been in. It had all seemed romantic back then. She'd thought of him as a hero, but he'd really been little more than a boy, a boy completely alone.

Bekka couldn't imagine growing up without both her parents and her noisy, boisterous, sometimes interfering, but well-meaning brothers and sister. More often than not, they drove her crazy, but she knew if she needed any one of them, or all of them, they'd be here, instantly, no questions asked. Well, maybe they'd ask a question or two, but frankly, she didn't know what she'd do without them.

"What did you do? After you left Millerton, I mean."

Conor condensed his history into three brief sentences. "I sort of laid low. I hung out and worked at whatever job I could find. Then Mac Pearson hired me, and I've been working in construction ever since." As an afterthought, he added, "There is a little of Mara in you, after all."

Conor shook his head in a way only men do when talking about a woman, and Bekka couldn't help but grin. His face was turned away from her, so she couldn't see that his mouth was touched with a faint smile, too.

Taking their glasses, she silently walked through the short hall and into the bathroom. While she rinsed the glasses beneath warm water, the medley of his mellow whistle reached her ears. She stood perfectly still at the bathroom sink, the warm water rushing over her fingers. She felt so mesmerized by the sound of him, she barely noticed the steaming water. Her heart thudded in her chest and tears ached behind her eyes. She didn't like feeling like this, so soft, so vulnerable. Feeling like this had a way of leading to heartache.

This powerful, unnameable emotion lurking between them threatened her control. The warm water streaming from the faucet became increasingly hot, and as the sudden stinging of her hands reached her subconscious, Bekka jerked them from the hot water. She placed a dripping hand to her neck and inhaled a deep breath of steamy air, meeting her eyes in her own reflection in the mirror.

He'd said he didn't know where home was. It wasn't his rented house. It wasn't the lot where he'd grown up.

It was strange that Conor hadn't known the lot was in his name. Bekka wondered who had paid for it all these years. If it hadn't been Conor, who could it be? He had no family, few friends. She stared at her own reflection as one person came to mind. Hands still dripping, Bekka spun around and ran back to the kitchen, a man's name already on her lips.

FIVE

"Vince Macelli," Bekka whispered the moment she reached the kitchen.

"What about him?" he asked, spacing the words out.

Surprise siphoned the blood from her face at the look on Conor's. "Vince was your friend. Don't you think he might have paid the taxes on your lot all these years?"

Conor held the tape measure in place with the toe of one work boot. He extended his arm as far as it would reach and marked the board with his carpenter's pencil. His voice, when he finally answered, was full of bitterness. "Give me one good reason why he'd do it."

"He *was* your best friend."

"*Was*, Bekka."

She tried to focus on the significance of his words and not on the way her heart swelled and her insides went soft because he'd murmured her name. "What happened, Conor? What ever happened to you and Vince? Why did you leave town so suddenly?"

A muscle moved at the edge of Conor's jaw, and

Bekka wished she hadn't asked about his past. She had no right to dredge up his pain, no right to expect an answer.

He stared down at the board he'd measured, and his answer was slow in coming. "You were right about Vince and me. He was my best friend. He changed that. And no matter how dilapidated my house was, at least I had a roof over my head. The fire changed that. So, I cleared out. As simple as that."

It wasn't as simple as that. There was a lot he wasn't telling her. Maybe he didn't want to relive the past. Bekka didn't blame him. She ached, as much for the lonesome boy he'd been as for the lonely man he'd become. "If you'd stayed, you could have dispelled the rumors about that fire."

"I didn't know people said *I* set fire to my own house. Bud Trierweller told me just this week."

"Oh, Conor, rumors can be so painful, more painful than the truth." Bekka hadn't realized she'd spoken out loud until he raised his gaze to hers. She hadn't been speaking about his pain, at least not entirely. The look of understanding in his eyes held her spellbound. He hadn't answered her question about what had happened between him and Vince, but at least now she knew why he'd left town.

"If Vince didn't pay those taxes, who did?" she asked.

"I don't know. Mac barked my head off when I accused him. There isn't anyone else. I just don't believe Macelli would have done it. What would he have to gain?"

It was Bekka's turn to shrug her shoulders. "It doesn't make sense."

He sighed, pulled his fingers through his hair, and made a sweeping glance at the torn up kitchen. When his gaze returned to hers, he said, "Nothing that's ever happened to me in Millerton has made a lot of sense."

Conor had worked in Detroit for twelve years, and nothing out of the ordinary had happened to him, aside from a couple of fistfights that first year and having his car stolen the second. No one had ever paid his taxes and no one mowed his grass but him. He'd been back in Millerton two months, and nothing made sense, certainly not the woman gazing at him with eyes darkened by emotion.

He'd known other women over the past twelve years and he'd had no trouble whatsoever keeping his mind on his work. He'd known Bekka less than one week and was powerless to resist her soft smiles.

If he was smart, he'd finish this kitchen and hightail it out of here. He'd resist her warmth and ignore what she did to his body. If he was smart, he wouldn't look into those soft blue eyes of hers, wouldn't let her smile sneak up on him, stinging his insides as sharply as a frown.

"Don't let Mara hear you say that about Millerton. Mike's great-great-grandfather founded this city, and she acts as if it all had something to do with her."

"She would." He didn't even try to hide his annoyance.

Bekka had no idea how the conversation had gotten to Mike's great-great-grandfather when she wanted to question Conor about his lot. "Even if you don't think Vince Macelli paid your taxes, I think we should talk to him about it."

"No!" That one syllable held more force than ten words.

"How else are we going to find the answer?"

"I don't know, but I'll come up with something."

"We," she said. "We'll come up with something,

Conor.'' Whether he knew it or not he wasn't alone anymore.

A wistfulness stole into his expression, and when he didn't argue the point, Bekka's only emotion was relief. Relief that she'd finally said it, and relief that he didn't turn her away.

The insistent ringing of the telephone a few feet away broke Conor's concentration. Stepping to the tall windows, he quickly scanned the backyard. As the phone rang a second time, he saw Bekka near the edge of her lawn riding back and forth as she mowed the grass. By the third ring he'd spied Jimmy and Jason in the garden, painstakingly watering their thirsty plants.

Conor grabbed the phone up midway through the fourth ring. ''Stevenson residence.''

For a moment he heard only silence. Then a feminine voice said, ''Conor?''

''Yes.''

''This is Mara. Hearing a man's voice answer Bekka's telephone made me momentarily speechless. That doesn't happen very often.''

He wondered what didn't happen often, a man answering Bekka's phone or Mara being struck speechless.

''Where is that sister of mine, anyway?''

''She's out back mowing the yard. The boys are in the garden . . .'' He was about to ask if he could take a message when Mara interrupted him.

''Listen, Conor, you don't have to go out and get Bekky right this minute. When she comes in, have her call me, okay? Tell her it's about the party she's having this weekend.''

He could practically hear her groan as she realized she'd mentioned the party. ''Um, you can come, too, Conor, if you want to, that is.''

Even though it had been little more than a token

invitation, he was surprised, and a little pleased, that Mara had made the attempt. He wondered what she'd do if he told her Bekka had already asked him to the party.

Bekka had been adamant about inviting him. She'd repeated the invitation three times and hadn't wanted to take no for an answer. The first time he'd turned her down with the excuse that he had work to do. The second time he was more evasive than negative, and the third time he'd simply said no thanks. As if she hadn't heard a word he'd said, she'd told him the invitation was open and he didn't have to decide right away.

"Conor?" Mara asked.

Conor turned at the sound of a door closing behind him. Bekka stood amid the unfinished wood of the new kitchen. Her hair was mussed, and her skin had taken on a tawny glow. He clenched his jaw against the knot in his stomach, the knot that had curled into a tight ball when Bekka had said *we*. She'd raised her chin and he knew Mara wasn't the only stubborn Taylor.

"Conor, are you still there?"

Without bothering to answer, he thrust the phone into Bekka's hands, mouthed the words "your sister," and strode outside.

"Hi, Mar," Bekka murmured on a sigh. The phone was still warm where it had rested against Conor's skin. That warmth filtered through the delicate lobe of her ear, and she became aware of the feelings of intimacy such a simple sharing created. She answered her sister's questions when appropriate and watched Conor out the window, her mind already beginning to wander.

The screaming saw drew her gaze, and Bekka wondered why they called them buzz saws when screech saws would be more accurate. Sawdust spun through the air like snowflakes, and a narrow piece of wood fell to the grass with a thud. Conor ran a block of sandpaper across the oak board and followed it with his palm. The man was a genius with a carpenter's pencil and a piece of wood.

Being near Conor was changing her. The changes were so subtle they were barely noticeable, yet they simmered just beneath her skin, shifting and weaving and rising at the oddest moments.

He claimed he was a loner, but she didn't believe him. He'd pretended indifference when she'd told him so, but his eyes had smoldered with another emotion. She didn't believe he wanted to be alone. He just didn't know any other way.

Bekka hung up the phone, carefully stepping over the thin sheets of lumber on the floor. Jimmy and Jason, empty watering cans swinging at their sides, walked from the garden, lost in conversation. She'd heard Jimmy cry out in his sleep the previous night, a deep, mournful wail that had jarred her awake and worried her long after she'd run to his bed, where he was already sound asleep. Seeing her sons together now warmed her heart. They, at least, knew they weren't alone. One way or another, she'd show Conor he wasn't alone either.

Later that afternoon Bekka decided telling Conor he wasn't alone was proving to be easier than showing him. With her kitchen out of commission, she'd promised the kids pizza for supper, but when she invited him along, he'd politely refused. She'd herded Jimmy and Jason through the shower and sent them to their room to change while she showered and dressed. Sharing the bathroom mirror with the boys, she brushed her hair and laughed when they tried to duck before she could brush theirs.

She followed the boys, her sandals clicking down the back stairs, across the kitchen's bare wood floor, and over the porch, where she drew herself up and, in a manner as casual as a shrug, invited Conor again. He looked intently at her and then at Jimmy and Jason.

"Hurry, Conor," Jason called. "Me and Jimmy are starved!"

Conor's face intrigued her, whether serious or thoughtful, but when he smiled, something, like hope, lighted in her chest. He shoved the saws to the front of the truck and clanked the tailgate shut. He unhooked the tool belt at his waist and strode around to the door. "Are you going to Antonio's?" he asked.

"Yes," Bekka and the boys called.

"I'll meet you there in twenty minutes." He climbed into the cab and closed the door. Through the open window, he said, "Don't wait for me to order. *We* wouldn't want those two to starve to death."

Bekka hesitated, confused by his unexpected response. Conor Bradley was not an easy man to second-guess. Not only had he accepted her invitation to dinner, he'd said *we*. Too bad convincing him to accept her invitation to Dustin's birthday party hadn't been as successful.

She raised her voice above his truck's noisy engine. "How do you like your pizza?"

Even though he didn't quite smile, there was something seductive in his look. His voice was low, his gaze steady. "Every way, Bekka. I like it every way."

She explored his eyes for hidden meaning and found plenty. It disturbed her and excited her and confused her. She'd been aware of his attraction from the beginning but lately had thought it was one-sided. Hers. She'd wanted to show him he wasn't alone, but the light in his eyes said he already knew it. He affected her, plain and simple.

He arrived at Antonio's twenty minutes later, before their pizza had arrived at the table. His dark hair was shower damp, and he'd exchanged his dusty jeans for a clean pair and his white T-shirt for a shirt with three buttons and a ribbed collar.

Someone fed quarters into the jukebox, and Bekka's heart beat with the pulse of the slow song. His blue eyes caught and held hers over the steaming pizza, and she had to look away. She automatically scooped a slice onto Jason's and Jimmy's plates, then did the same to hers and Conor's. Eating gave her something to do, and Jimmy and Jason gave her someplace else to look.

The boys dug into their pizza with reckless abandon. Conor raised his eyebrows and did the same.

"Wow," Jason piped. "You must really like pizza, Conor!"

"You weren't the only ones starving," he returned.

"Is pizza your favorite food?" Jimmy asked, the first time he'd spoken since Conor's arrival.

"It's up there near the top."

Without bothering to empty his mouth, Jason asked, "Did our daddy like pizza, Mommy?"

Jimmy didn't wait for Bekka's answer. "Everyone likes pizza, you dummy."

"Mindy doesn't," Jason declared.

"She's a girl," Jimmy stated. "All boys like pizza."

"Marc doesn't," Jason argued.

"Marc's just a baby."

Bekka's reaction to Jason's question had been swift. She rarely talked about the boys' father, and they rarely asked. She didn't know how much to tell them, so she told them very little. "Guys, a lot of people like pizza, but it has nothing to do with being a boy or a girl, and Jason, your father liked it but not as much as you do."

Conor had felt the change in the atmosphere the moment the younger boy had asked about his father. Jason didn't appear all that interested. He just seemed to be making conversation. But Jimmy and Bekka had both reacted instantaneously. Her answer had satisfied Jason, but Jimmy remained pensive.

Conor didn't claim to know the first thing about kids, but he knew something was going on in Jimmy's head. And in Bekka's. Whatever it was, it was still in the backs of their minds as they finished their pizza, was still there ten minutes later when they pulled up to the curb behind him.

Leaning against the truck, Conor watched as Jason pushed the car door open and jumped to the ground, Jimmy right behind him. Why he'd suggested coming here, he hadn't a clue. But as he watched the kids run across the vacant lot, he realized he wasn't sorry he had. The excitement of exploring an open lot chased Jimmy's pensiveness away. Conor wasn't sure what had chased away Bekka's.

The evening breeze blew the mugginess from the late June air and blew the softly gathered material of her skirt against her legs and hips. Her skirt was flowered in creams and yellows, the top the same, simple in its design, sleeveless, and scoop necked. But the way the material lay against her skin, flowing over her breasts and cinched into the skirt's waistband, made it exquisite. He wondered if she had any idea what a captivating picture she made, wondered if she had any idea how badly he wanted to touch her.

She'd told him he wasn't alone. But he was, and so was she. They were just alone, together.

"Mommy! Look at me!" Jason called from the back of the property.

Without a word, Bekka and Conor slowly made their way toward the kids. Halfway there, she murmured, "I remember this yard."

She looked up at him, and the wind lifted her hair from her shoulders. The glow of her smile touched his memory, and he knew he'd seen that smile before. Not yesterday, or last week, but a long time ago. She'd been kind to him, when he could count the kindness he'd received that year on one hand.

The memory shook him. He stopped walking and noticed she had, too. "You were here that night." That night his world, what there was of it, fell apart.

"I didn't think you remembered."

"I didn't until now."

Bekka sensed his anguish, just as she'd sensed it twelve years ago. She turned her head, speaking into the breeze. "I didn't expect you to remember me. I mean, it was a long time ago, and I was only sixteen."

It may have been a long time ago, but she'd never forgotten a single detail of that night. She'd been out with her girlfriends when they saw him lying motionless on the grass near the sidewalk. She told Amy Parker, the girl driving, to pull up to the curb. The others didn't get out, but Bekka had. She'd helped him up, helped him into the house. She'd looked into his eyes, and she'd never forgotten the desolation she'd seen there.

She'd seen that kind of desolation only one other time—the night Ted left, the same night he died.

"Mom, look at us!" Jimmy called. If it hadn't been for the patch of orange peeking between the leafy branches, she wouldn't have known they were in the tree. She could hear Jimmy's voice prodding his younger brother to the next branch and Jason's voice quaver, "O-kay."

"Don't climb too high," she called.

She and Conor walked to the back of the lot and stood beneath the tree, looking up. The boys were straddling a branch like a horse, lost in play. Bekka's gaze followed Conor's stare. She took a step toward him and, with her finger, traced the initials carved into the tree.

"Conor Bradley, number one," he whispered.

She captured his eyes with hers. Her voice, when it came, was rose-petal soft. "Who gave you that black eye that night?" When he didn't answer, she said, "Vince Macelli?"

"Yeah."

Biting her lip, she looked away. Bekka understood why Conor didn't believe Vince had paid those taxes, but she wasn't entirely convinced he hadn't. He could have paid them all these years. Out of guilt. Vince had knocked his best friend out with his bare hands. He'd severed the friendship, and she didn't believe either of them had healed.

"What are you going to do with this land?" she asked.

"I'm going to build a house."

"Conor, that's wonderful!" Her smile broadened in approval. "When did you decide to do that?"

"About ten seconds ago."

She laughed at his surprise. "What kind of house are you going to build?"

"One made from bricks, solid and sturdy and strong."

She looked into his face, but he wasn't looking her way. He was staring at the initials in the tree, and she didn't want to intrude on his thoughts, so she didn't utter the words on her tongue. She didn't tell him he was going to build a house just like him. Solid and sturdy and strong.

The yard was neatly mowed, the grass lush and thick. Her flowers bloomed in a profuse display of color, the rich soil freshly tilled. The top porch step gave Bekka a bird's-eye view of the backyard, where loud shouts and hoots were evidence that the party was well under way.

Everything was perfect. Well, almost everything.

Conor wasn't among the people gathering in the backyard.

She didn't understand herself. Nor could she understand Conor. She'd felt his eyes upon her these past few days. Her skin would tingle, her heart thudding with an awakening emotion. Then, just as quickly, he'd turn away, leaving her heartbeat to return to normal.

"Come on, Bekka," Mara bossed. "We need a line coach and scorekeeper."

"Mara, I'm the one with the torn up kitchen. Why do these parties always end up in my backyard?"

"Because you have the perfect place for parties," Mara answered.

"That's not what you said when you first saw this house," Bekka reminded her.

"I said it was drafty, would be a lot of work, and was in the country. Was I wrong?"

Bekka didn't grace her sister with a reply. Instead, she turned her attention to the group of family and friends assembled for the party. "Where are the kids tonight?" Dustin asked.

Walking toward the net, Bekka answered, "Mara said Missy was a little feverish, so she left all three of them with Mike's parents for the evening. And Jimmy and Jason were invited to a friend's house, one with a swimming pool, and I'm afraid they'd rather go swimming than watch a bunch of adults play volleyball."

They'd divided into teams, and the first game of volleyball noisily began. Dustin, being the gallant guest of honor at his birthday celebration, had the first serve. He'd brought a few friends along, and his serve, having barely made it over the net, was met with friendly sarcasm. From that point on, the game continued in haphazard earnestness.

Since there was an uneven number of players, a different person was deemed to sit out each game. That person became designated line coach and scorekeeper. For this game that person happened to be Bekka.

She stood on the sidelines and good-naturedly kept score. When she saw dust rolling in the distance, she forgot which team was ahead. When she saw that the vehicle stirring up the dusty gravel was a brown Chevy, she left the volleyball players to keep track of their own scores and hurried to her driveway.

Conor stepped down from the running board wearing tan pleated shorts, a white shirt, and a guarded smile. Sunglasses hid his eyes from Bekka's gaze. Although she couldn't see through the dark lenses, she knew the exact moment he picked Vince Macelli from the group of players around the net.

Conor's body language spoke volumes. For a moment she thought he was going to leave, without a word, without a backward glance. Boisterous whoops coming from the game covered her erratic heartbeat. She didn't want him to go but didn't know what to say to convince him to stay.

"He came with Dusty," she murmured. "I didn't know."

For a moment he didn't move. As if reaching a decision, he took a deep breath and said, "You might as well introduce me to your family and friends."

She looked up at the hard lines of his face, the angled cheekbones and firm jawline. His eyes were the one feature that could soften his bold looks. She wished he'd take those sunglasses off, wished he'd at least look at her.

Even though he'd given her no indication that he'd come to the party tonight, she should have known better than to try to second-guess him. She wondered what had changed his mind, what had brought him here when he'd so adamantly refused.

"I'm glad you came."

Conor finally looked at her, and she knew the exact moment he accepted her smile, her welcome. A wistfulness stole into his expression, and he gave her a guarded smile of his own.

Together they walked to the backyard, where the winners were gloating and the losers were talking of retaliation. Everyone was digging for cold pop through ice-filled coolers. Bekka began the introductions, while one of Dusty's friends sputtered, "Conor Bradley? No kidding? I remember you. My older brother used to call you and Macelli Butch Cassidy and the Sundance Kid."

For a moment the crowd went still. Everyone seemed to hold his breath while Vince and Conor stared at each other, each of their gazes hidden behind dark glasses.

Mara saved the day, completely changing the subject. "So, Dusty," she quipped, "where's your date?"

The guests seemed to breathe a sigh of relief, readily turning their attention to Dustin Taylor. It took Conor and Vince a moment longer to recover than the rest.

One of Dusty's friends said, "His date is probably washing her hair."

Another taunted, "He dates women with hair?"

Amusement flowed through the crowd. There was elbow jabbing and a fair share of laughter at Dustin's expense as the guests attempted to cool down after the first heated round of volleyball. One of the friends shouted, "It's rough for Dustin, ya know? He insists that he only dates women whose names begin with the letter *d*. Dusty here has slim pickings enough without that added qualification."

"Dusty, why would you have difficulty with women?" his mother asked.

Dustin's father threw his hands into the air in mock exasperation, and Bekka looked for Conor's reaction to her family. For a moment his guard was down and she thought he was going to laugh. Then his head turned in Vince's direction, and tension overtook his expression.

Dustin addressed the group. "I'd just like to thank everyone, especially you, Mara, for coming tonight and for bringing my social life, or the lack of a social life, to everyone's attention. I don't know how to thank you."

"Think nothing of it, Dusty. What are sisters for?"

Someone shouted, "Let's play ball!" And the guests once again assembled around the net. With Conor's arrival both teams were evenly numbered. Bekka was certain Conor's and Vince's choices of opposing teams hadn't been accidental.

For the first time since he arrived, the sharp-edged anxiety in Conor's chest dulled. He hadn't planned to come tonight, and when he saw Macelli there in the backyard, he wished he wouldn't have. He'd come because Bekka had invited him, not once, but three times, because he wanted to see her, and because he couldn't stay away.

The players had rotated positions, and he found himself directly behind Bekka. Her hair was fastened in a loose knot on top of her head, allowing his eyes access to her fine-boned neck. She was slender and agile, and when she hit the ball, muscles were evident in her upper arms.

Her red shorts only hinted at the curves hidden beneath. Her shirt was sleeveless, the same color as her shorts. It was trimmed with some sort of delicately woven thread and reached just to her waist. When she raised her arms to hit the volleyball, a patch of smooth skin was bared. That pale skin drew his gaze and Conor nearly missed the setup shot. A different kind of tension gathered in his chest before slowly sinking to his stomach.

She was an avid volleyball player. She didn't flinch

as she set the ball up straight into the air so that Conor could drive it back over to the opposing side. The other teams grunted and groaned as Bekka's team spiked the final ball over the net for a wide victory.

Everyone sauntered back nearer to the house. Mara's husband, Mike, flopped down in the soft grass beneath the shade of a large maple tree. "I'm getting too old for this."

Mara carefully lowered herself next to her husband. She breathed deeply and, wrapping her arms about her abdomen, doubled over in pain. Mike instantly raised to his elbow, a worried frown creasing his face. "Have you been having more of those pains?"

"This is the first time today. But they seem to be getting worse," she whispered.

"What pains, Mar?" Bekka asked.

"Oh, it's nothing . . ."

Mike interrupted his wife. "She's been having pains for the last few days."

Emma Taylor was suddenly on the scene, her cool hand pressed to her daughter's forehead in the age-old fashion of mothers everywhere. "You do feel a little warm. Your father and I were going to the lake tomorrow morning. We'd better postpone our plans," Emma thought out loud.

"Mother, I'm fine. Really! Don't change your plans because of me. I just have a little bug, just little pains. I'm sure it's nothing. See, I'm feeling better already." Mara clearly didn't like all the fuss she was causing.

Conor witnessed the intuitive exchanges between these family members in silent fascination. They were *kind* to each other. The kindnesses he'd received as a child had been fleeting. He couldn't imagine what it must have been like to grow up within this volatile family. Bekka may not appreciate their interference, but what a sense of belonging each member must feel.

Vince was also watching the scene, and Conor wondered if he, too, felt the lack of kindness, even now. But then, Vince had had a mother, and although she'd never won any medals for mother of the year, she had been good, in her own way, to her only son. She'd been one of the few people to bestow warmth on her son's best friend. The lady at the candy counter in the drugstore had been another, and one of his teachers in high school had tried to mother him, but by then he'd become independent.

Bekka caught his eye and smiled, and something deep inside him responded. Kindness hurt. He'd known it as a child. He knew it now.

From the corner of his eye he watched Vince Macelli. Bekka had wanted to ask Vince about that lot, but watching him in the distance, Conor didn't believe he'd paid those taxes. Vince seemed to have recovered from their childhoods. He was a policeman for goodness sake. He seemed to have many friends, although, as far as Conor knew, he hadn't found the right woman. In that respect, they were both alone.

Vince shook Dustin's hand, and Dusty said, "You're leaving already?"

"I'm filling in for one of the guys on the night shift," Vince answered. He raised his voice and called good night to everyone. His gaze slid over Conor, then back again, as he stared at him a moment longer than the rest. Squaring his shoulders, he turned and walked away.

Tension dug in between Conor's shoulder blades, and he suddenly felt the need for a long, hard run, the longer and harder the better. A small group of men had gathered near him, and the conversation turned to comfortable topics, like lumber and family room additions and the house he was planning to build on his lot.

Todd Taylor, Bekka's older brother, flipped the volleyball into the air before stuffing it inside his shirt, mimicking his wife's proportions. Tammy playfully jabbed her husband in the ribs as she said, "At least I have good reason for my evident weight gain. To what do you attribute your food cravings?"

Conor scrutinized Bekka's family. All four Taylor siblings were blond, like their mother, but Mara was the only one with her build. Bekka and her brothers took after their father's frame. He had a long, lean body, except for a little middle-aged paunch, and a look shrewd enough to rival Mara's.

Todd, Mara, and Frank didn't seem to agree on anything, from politics to how many burgers to grill. As conversation flowed around him, Conor watched Bekka quietly leave them to their argument, unobtrusively slapping burgers onto the double gas grill. She'd flipped them and her mother had seasoned each burger by the time the other three had agreed on an even three dozen.

"Two dozen," Bekka said.

"Two dozen burgers will never be enough," Todd chided.

Tammy shook her head and rolled her eyes heavenward. Emma Taylor pointed her salt shaker at her eldest son, and Conor knew where Bekka had gotten her firm voice, the one that left no room for argument. "Todd Alexander Taylor, we've never run out of food, and I doubt we'll start tonight."

Food was set out, the table practically groaning beneath the weight of the feast it supported. Plates were filled and everyone sat down to enjoy the food, the fresh air, and the camaraderie of family and friends.

Bekka found the last empty space, placed her plate on the picnic table, and dropped onto the bench. Noisy laughter and rumbling conversation dimmed in her ears as she found herself staring into Conor's face. He'd removed his sunglasses, and the look in his eyes held her spellbound. His gaze traveled over her face, touching upon her eyes, her cheeks, and her mouth. The smoldering flame she saw in his eyes found its way inside her.

She glanced around the table and found her father and Mara watching her. She turned her attention to the meal, but the thick juicy burger had lost its appeal. Their eyes held worry and a hint of censure.

When everyone had finished eating and the tables were cleared, the guests reassembled around the net for another game of volleyball. "Emma, why don't you and I sit this one out?" Frank said, stretching comfortably in the shade at the picnic table.

Bekka exchanged a few words with her mother, then veered off toward the other players. Mara fell into step on her right, Todd on her left. *Look out, here it comes*, she thought to herself.

"Bekka, what do you think you're doing?" Mara spoke first, but the expression in Todd's eyes mirrored Mara's.

Bekka had been aware of their scrutiny all evening and wasn't surprised at their reaction, but she'd thought they'd wait until after the party to voice their concerns.

"Bek," Todd declared, "Kathleen Ramsey told me she saw you and Bradley in Antonio's last night."

"She's kissed him, Todd," Mara quipped.

Todd let his breath out on a deep sigh. "I just hope you know what you're doing."

Bekka didn't answer, didn't favor them with so much as a glance. Dustin called to them from the backyard, and Bekka snatched her opportunity for escape. She could have told them they didn't need to worry, that no matter how much pizza she and Conor shared, something kept them from sharing more, something deep inside him, and something deep inside her.

This time she and Conor played side by side. There

were four fewer players and the other team was playing to win. Both teams had scored several points, but Bekka's team was trailing by four. Dustin served the ball, hitting it hard, sending it flying fast and high in the air to Bekka's side of the net.

Conor, Todd, and Bekka all yelled, "I've got it!" and all three came together with a hollow thud. Bekka tumbled to the grass, Conor and Todd toppling onto her as the ball bounced to the ground behind them. Air swooshed from Bekka's lungs as the weight of these two men piled on top of her slight form. Todd rolled off with a groan and Conor said, "Are you all right?"

His voice was husky, his breath tickling her ear. His legs straddled hers intimately, the hair of his muscular calves brushing hers. He rolled to his knees and she sat up dazedly. Her heart was beating rapidly, and she knew it wasn't due to the hard tumble to the ground.

One of Dusty's friends shouted, "No tackling, you guys! This isn't football, you know."

The crowd laughed, their chortled hoots ringing in the summer air. Todd and Conor each extended a hand to help Bekka to her feet. She looked from one face to the other. Todd wore a knowing look, and Conor's expression was closed. She quickly inserted a hand into each of theirs, and they pulled her to her feet so easily she practically flew through the air. That light, airy feeling remained long after her feet were back on the ground.

The game continued, but Bekka couldn't rid herself of the memory of Conor's body pressed to hers. Her mind refused to follow the game and she missed easy plays.

Conor was having his own difficulties. It was taking all his willpower to keep his hormones in check. This smoldering attraction between him and Bekka was turning into more. He wondered how much longer his body could withstand the onslaught of unrequited desire, and in the end, his team lost.

The women sauntered to the sidelines, and the men decided it was time to play real ball. Shirts were pulled off and tossed to the sidelines. The ball was spiked and pounded back and forth over the high net. Each of the players jumped like pros, and Bekka knew more than a few of them would be sore in the morning.

The red-orange sun was setting low in the western sky, seeming to rest atop a dark green woods in the distance. Intense thumps and thuds and grunts overtook the natural evening quiet as the men bombarded the defenseless volleyball with their arms and fists.

The women pulled up lawn chairs and huddled a short distance away. Bekka's chair was angled a foot behind the others and she leaned back to watch the game taking place before her. Some of the plays were comical as the men dove headfirst to keep the ball from touching the ground. The women smiled and joked, but Bekka was silent, her eyes on one man.

SIX

A layer of perspiration, touched with the orange gleam of the sun, glistened over Conor's upper torso. When he lifted his arms to slam the ball, muscles raised beneath his skin and seemed to roll across his broad shoulders and down his back. That airy sensation that had settled in her midsection when they'd toppled to the ground was now replaced with a new heaviness. Bekka crossed her legs, but the action did little to relieve the pressure deep in her body.

Conor leaped into the air, pounding the ball back to the other side before landing on the hard ground, his feet springing back to earth. He had the long, muscular legs of a runner. Dark hair curled on his calves, and on his chest too, but not thickly, so that Bekka could see his skin underneath.

By the time the game ended the sun had dropped behind the trees far in the distance, making it difficult to see the small white ball. Conor bent to retrieve his shirt from the ground. He straightened, and his eyes locked with Bekka's.

She'd been watching him. That knowledge made him

want to show off for her benefit. Instead, he shrugged into his shirt and strode to her side. He felt an indefinable feeling of confidence and fought the urge to entwine Bekka's fingers in his, to pull her to his side.

"Congratulations!" she murmured after taking a sip from the can of cola she held.

"These men play for blood."

"That's my family. Competitive to a fault."

The words were innocent enough, but the longing in their gazes wasn't. Conor took the can from her grasp, brushing his thumb over her soft fingertips. He raised it to his dry lips, took a long swallow, and returned it to her open hand.

Without waiting for her quickened pulse to subside, she placed the can to her parted lips, touching them to the spot where his had just been. It was an intimate gesture, as intimate as a kiss, but not nearly as satisfying.

Coolers and lawn chairs were gathered up and carried to the trunks of cars as the guests prepared to leave. Dustin and his friends left, and the other couples gradually did the same. Mara, in her weakened state, allowed Mike to lead her off without a word, but Todd wasn't as easily persuaded. He and his father must have read the desire in Conor's eyes, because they did their best to outlast him. In the end Tammy pleaded a backache, and Emma finally dragged Frank away.

Conor and Bekka were alone. The sky that had been streaked with purple and pink only moments before was suddenly without color as night once again touched the earth with darkness. Creatures of the night suddenly came to life as flying insects flitted and unknown animals scuttled through the underbrush of the nearby fields.

Conor leaned his hip against the picnic table, and Bekka leaned against the porch railing, her back to the house. A single lamp glowed from a window in the family room, the only light in the entire house.

The large house beckoned to him, and he wanted to swing her into his arms and carry her inside and . . . There were so many things he wanted to do to her, with her. He knew where he wanted it to end, and he knew where he wanted to begin. With a touch, a caress.

She pushed herself from the rail and sauntered toward him, the look in her eyes gripping his heart with tenderness, his thoughts gripping the rest of him with longing. "Where are the kids tonight?" He wanted to kiss her, and he didn't want to be interrupted.

"They're spending the night with friends." She'd answered his question without thinking, because, at that moment, she was incapable of coherent thought. One by one, stars twinkled into view high in the sky as both of them, standing far below, battled with their own thoughts.

Dew was settling to the ground, the subtle moistness cooling Bekka's skin. Her nerve endings were jumpy, her awareness of Conor so intense. Her desire to be close to this man was growing, and her feelings had nothing to do with reason. She remembered the look in her father's eyes and in Todd's and Mara's. It reminded Bekka of another time, of a heartache she thought she'd never get over. They'd been right that time. What if they were right again?

Conor sensed her anticipation, her honest affection. Most of all he sensed her desire. It practically sparked in the air between them. But the eyes looking intently at him weren't bright with passion. She looked away hastily, as if fears and uncertainties, older than time itself, had been resurrected.

A warning voice whispered in his head, and he held his raw emotions in check. After a moment, he whispered, "You have quite a family."

Bekka saw his wry smile and reminded herself it wasn't Conor's fault her family tried to run her life. They always had, and she'd always resisted. Nearly every decision she'd made had proved to be right. Except for one. Her decision to marry Ted Stevenson was her single irreversible decision-making flop. She'd learned to live with the consequences of that decision a long time ago. Two of those consequences, Jason and Jimmy, were the joy of her life, and creating a home for them was her reason for living.

"Bekka?" Conor's voice pulled at her thoughts, pulled her gaze to his. It was all she could do to meet the question in his eyes. "I understand about shadows, Bekka. Tell me about yours."

Before her stood a man who'd grown up alone, was alone still. She'd never thought he was a man of delicate scruples, yet here he was offering something he'd never received, a part of himself, a part she doubted he'd ever offered before.

He didn't attempt to hide the fact that he was watching her. His eyes appeared dark, his expression guarded, as if he thought she'd refuse him. In that moment, she doubted she could have refused him anything.

Bekka wanted to tell him about her shadows but didn't know where to begin. She rarely thought about Ted anymore, and she hadn't shared her feelings about him and their past with anyone in years. For the first time in a long, long time, she wanted to tell someone about him. Not just anyone. She wanted to tell Conor.

Conor gave her time to organize her thoughts, watching as she propped her hip against the table, facing him across the short arm's-length distance that separated them. Airy wisps of hair had fallen from the loosened knot on her head, touching the nape of her neck and shoulders the way he wanted to.

She was reluctant to open an old wound, and he

didn't blame her. Talking about the past, especially when the past was painful, wasn't easy. He expected her to begin with her husband, how they met, or at least how he'd died. Instead she began with her sister.

"I'm twenty-eight years old, and fourteen months older than Mara, but ever since she uttered her first word, she's been trying to run my life along with her own. And Todd isn't much better. He's just more subtle. Then there's my father with all his knowing looks . . ."

Her voice trailed away, and Conor wondered what her family had to do with her husband. She seemed resigned to their interference, pensive rather than angry. This was one facet of her character he'd never seen before.

"They've always tried to run your life?" At her nod, he asked, "Did they warn you about your husband?"

Her gaze traveled up the wall of his flat stomach, grazing his neck, settling to his mouth. She wet her lips, and he tried to ignore the pulsing knot that had formed in his stomach. Conor prided himself on the durability of his willpower, but resisting her was becoming increasingly difficult. He kept his distance, when what he wanted to do was kiss her moist lips.

Her eyes strayed from his, and he wondered if, looking into the shadows of her garden, she was seeing her husband amid the shadows of her past. After a moment, she began. "Ted was wonderful. And horrible, and for four years, he was the man I loved."

She'd loved him. Even now, years later, she knew it was true. "I met him in college, looked into his eyes across a crowded room, and fell instantly in love. When I brought him home, I didn't understand what Todd and Mara could possibly have against him. Mom and Dustin's caution was more difficult to ignore."

"They didn't like him?"

"It wasn't that. It's just that they saw something I

didn't see. They saw his aloofness as distant, I saw it as endearing. I loved him. Maybe I didn't want to see."

"But you married him anyway."

"Yes," she whispered. "And at first I was so happy with him. He knew exactly what he wanted in life, and I was in love with a dream, a dream I thought we both shared. Unfortunately, we didn't want the same things. By the time we discovered those differences it was too late."

"Too late?"

Her voice dropped to barely more than a whisper. "We'd only been married a year when I learned I was expecting Jimmy. I was thrilled. He wasn't."

"He didn't want to start a family so soon?" Conor asked, trying to understand why the birth of a baby, even an unplanned birth, would have been so unfortunate for a married couple.

"Ted didn't want to start a family. Ever. I had no idea he felt that way, and although Jimmy came along sooner than I'd planned, I wanted him. I knew my pregnancy would make my last year of college more difficult, but I thought Ted and I would adjust. Jimmy's arrival strained our marriage beyond belief. Jason's untimely arrival thirteen months later broke it completely."

Conor understood what it was like to grow up unwanted, and he finally understood why the look in Jimmy's eyes had reminded him of himself. "Do Jimmy and Jason remember their father?"

"I don't think so. But sometimes, when I look into Jimmy's eyes, I wonder."

"What do you think he remembers?" Conor asked. Something almost tangible sliced through him at the pain etched in her gaze.

"How could he remember?" she whispered. "He was only two when his father died. Jason wasn't even one."

There was something she wasn't telling him. Something she'd seen, something that still worried her, haunted her.

"They rarely ask about him. The other night in Antonio's was the first time in as long as I can remember. I told them their father left us enough money to buy this house, that he is providing for his two sons even though he can't be with them."

"Is this the type of house he would have wanted?" Conor asked.

"No," she murmured, closing her eyes against the truth. "I'll never tell them this is the last kind of home Ted would have wanted. Some things are better left unsaid."

Conor clenched his jaw. In his mind he built the image she portrayed of Ted. It wasn't a pretty picture. No wonder he'd sensed the weight of responsibility she single-handedly carried.

"So, you moved back to your hometown and bought this old house and are being forced to deal with interference from your family."

She opened her eyes in surprise. "You make their interference sound frivolous!" She stared wordlessly at him. When he cast a sidelong glance at her face, she saw a look of such tenderness in his expression it amazed her.

"Not frivolous, Bekka. What I saw of your family tonight didn't look frivolous. It looked blessed. They mean well, and you seem to handle them. You live your own life in spite of their interference."

He said her life looked blessed. Bekka basked in the knowledge of his surprising belief in her determination. It warmed her voice, buoyed her spirits. "Yes."

Hadn't she always known she had powerful conviction? Some people would call it a stubborn streak, but it was a natural element of her complex personality, one that Ted never appreciated. Ted wasn't standing before her tonight. Conor was. And she realized he not only accepted her stubborn streak, he seemed to respect her for it. She hadn't realized, until that moment, how much his respect meant to her.

She didn't know what else to say, and they were each lost for a moment in their own thoughts, so that all they heard was the hushed stillness in the quiet night. She wanted to thank him for listening, but she was afraid he would misconstrue her gratitude for admiration.

His presence at the party tonight had further awakened her awareness of him as a man. When he was near, Bekka became aware of her own needs. His presence worked magic on her senses. Instinctively, she reacted to him, both physically and emotionally.

Her head ached from the battles taking place within her, the battles between her mind and her body. And Bekka realized that she was lonely. She'd learned to live with loneliness, even before Ted had died, but she knew there was one thing she couldn't deal with. Another broken heart.

"Conor, I'm glad you decided to come to the party tonight."

He sensed a *but* was coming. She'd closed the book of her past in the middle of an important chapter. But after listening to even that small bit, he better understood her reluctance to admit their awakening desire.

Without saying a word, he lowered his head to hers. He heard her gasp, felt her breath catch in her throat, but her eyes remained half opened. He barely grazed her lips, and she parted them slightly. He didn't slide his fingers into her hair, didn't pull her closer. He took the kiss a step farther, and he felt her lashes flutter closed against his cheek. A delicate thread seemed to pull them together, but in reality, neither moved closer.

She tilted her head a little to one side, and he felt the heady sensation of her lips moving against his. This wasn't a passionate kiss as the other one they'd shared had been. This was simply a whispered promise of what could be.

Conor lingered a moment longer, then straightened. She opened her eyes, and he saw starlight reflected in their depths. His voice, when he found it, was low and husky. "I'll see you Monday morning. Sweet dreams, Bekka."

She watched as he walked to his truck, saw him retrieve something from the floor, and was almost sure she saw him stiffen. He drove away into the darkness of the country night, and Bekka felt a piece of her heart go with him.

Once inside her home, the doors all safely bolted against the unknown elements of the dark, she wandered from room to room. Her big house was strangely quiet. The complete silence was unsettling. She realized it was partly because Jason and Jimmy weren't sleeping peacefully in their beds upstairs. It was also partly because of Conor.

Bekka thought about how quickly her little ones were growing. Almost overnight they had grown from babies to little boys, and she was sure they would grow into men just as quickly. Men like Conor. Strong, honest, and sincere.

How easily she'd opened her past for his brief view. After reminiscing about her late husband, she believed her thoughts would have centered on him. But images of Ted were fleeting. The man drifting through her thoughts was tall and dark, intense and alluring. The name whispering through her mind was Conor.

She'd known him for less than two weeks, mere days really, yet he'd filtered through her resolve to remain uninvolved the way the summer breeze filtered through the lacy curtains covering her bedroom windows. The curtains ruffling on the silent, invisible air mimicked the wavering emotions thoughts of Conor evoked.

Bekka placed her hands to her cheeks, letting a long sigh escape her lips, and walked barefoot into the tiny upstairs bathroom. After brushing her teeth, she splashed her face with warm water. Staring at her reflection in the mirror, she loosened the knot of hair at the top of her head, the light tendrils falling to her shoulders.

Smoothing the tangle of hair with slow strokes of her brush, she finished preparing for bed. Bekka crawled between the freshly laundered sheets and stretched her legs over the entire expanse of the large bed. She'd slept alone in this bed for five years. Why did she suddenly feel lonely.

Memories of Conor's kiss refused to budge from her mind. She tossed and turned and tried to think of something, anything, else. How many nights had she fallen asleep imagining what her home would look like when another remodeling project was completed? Thinking about her house couldn't chase the thoughts of Conor away. Even counting sheep didn't help. Their bleating baa-baa repeatedly turned into Conor's voice quietly calling, "Bekka, Bekka."

As much as she tried to prevent it, the last swirling thoughts of wakefulness revolved around Conor and the pleasing certainty that in him she had discovered something wonderful. Her eyes slowly fluttered closed and she drifted into a peaceful sleep.

Conor turned the key, and the truck's engine went quiet. It had been only five minutes since he'd left Bekka's. Five minutes since he'd found the note. The street lamp didn't penetrate the darkness in the cab of the truck, didn't glint off the plain white paper laying on the seat next to him.

Leave. Or else.

The words had been handwritten, in sloppy, mismatched letters. There was no salutation, no signature, but the message was clear, painfully so. Someone didn't want him here.

He had no idea how long the note had been on the floor of his truck. It could have been days. It could have been minutes. Nor did he know who had put it there. It could have been someone at tonight's party, or it could have been someone else entirely.

The only thing threatening about the note was the unknown. Who wanted him to leave? And why? What had he ever done to make someone hate him, enough to demand that he leave?

He'd left town once. Even though he'd been young then, and bone tired, he'd left of his own free will. He'd done nothing wrong, nothing except being born to the town drunk and a young girl in trouble. He left that night because a fire had destroyed his house, and Vince's fury had severed their friendship. Conor didn't blame Vince for his rage. What Sam Bradley had done sickened Conor even now. But Vince had destroyed their friendship for the sins of Conor's father.

Conor understood Jason's curiosity about his father. Good or bad, sons looked for a connection to the man who's sired them. He'd come to terms with his feelings for his own father years ago. He'd loved him at first, and hated him later, and in the end, he'd pitied him. If a person believed in just rewards, Conor figured his father had gotten his. After the fire Sam Bradley had climbed into the backseat of Conor's car and fallen asleep. At a stoplight in downtown Detroit he crawled out again, saying, "Looks like we're even, kid." He'd died alone in a seedy hotel the year after he'd left Millerton.

His father had given him three things, his height, a

roof over his head, such as it was, and now, inadvertently, that vacant lot. The rest, Conor knew, was up to him, just as it had always been.

"Mommy, can I get this one?" Jason asked. Seated at the low table in the children's section of the local library, he held a book up for his mother to inspect.

Bekka barely heard him. She was systematically pulling books from a high shelf across the room. After leafing through several, she reinserted them, one by one, onto the shelf before pulling another.

"Mommy . . . Mom-my!" Jason persisted.

"Hmmm?" she absently turned toward her son's insistent voice penetrating her concentration.

"Can I get this one?" he repeated.

Lowering her voice to a whisper, Bekka said, "Yes, honey, you may choose three. But don't forget, we should whisper when we're in a library."

In a distinctly pronounced whisper, her younger son said, "Okay. Jimmy, don't forget ya hafta whisper." Bekka smiled as she turned her attention back to her selection.

Once, a few years ago, while she'd been searching for ideas for remodeling her home, she came across a book about old, refurbished Detroit houses. She'd remembered the book Saturday night in her dreams. Conor had told her he'd worked in the suburbs of Detroit for nearly twelve years, and she wanted to show him that book. Who knows, maybe he'd seen those houses, maybe he'd even worked on one or two of them?

There it is! Pulling the book from its hiding place on the top shelf, she quickly leafed through its contents. A smile broadened her lips as she imagined his delight. She signed the card from the book's back pocket and waited while Jimmy and Jason chose their reading material. Looking around at the familiar sight of the small public library, she inhaled the musty scent of old, well-read books.

Nestled in a portion of an old building, the library was just around the corner from the main street. The place had changed little over the years. High ceilings and worn wooden floors supported row upon row of book-covered shelves.

She'd come here often with Jimmy and Jason these past five years. Bekka thought about the countless times she'd walked up and down these aisles, leisurely helping them choose books to read. But this morning, she didn't feel leisurely. She was in a hurry to get home. To Conor. She'd shared her past with him. He'd kissed her, and there was a subtle difference in the beating rhythm of her heart. She felt lighthearted, changed, on the brink of something new.

Sweet dreams, Bekka. The sound of his voice still echoed inside her head. He'd murmured those words two nights ago, and for two days her thoughts had echoed with that deep voice, for two nights her dreams had been filled with Conor.

The moment her eyes had opened shortly after dawn, the memory of her dreams escaped her, but she awoke with a smile and as she listened to the early morning songs of birds joyfully proclaiming another morning, she was anxious to begin this new day. That smile returned at the oddest moments, her brain unable to prevent the image of Conor's dark blue gaze and slow smile and firm, hard body from rippling across the screen of her mind.

With uncharacteristic impatience, she'd waited in line at the grocery store. Even though she'd tried to hurry, it was late morning by the time she and the boys climbed back into the car and headed for home, the week's groceries stashed in the trunk of her car, library books clutched in their hands.

Bekka turned into her driveway, slowly curving around the oak tree, its wide, leaf-covered branches dappling the gravel with shade. Pulling in front of the garage, she slid the lever into park and turned the key. The low, laborious hum of her car's air conditioner suddenly ceased.

She was home.

As always, that first glimpse of the black shingled roof that covered the expanse of the second story and protected the rambling porches magnetized her. The glass-paned windows reflected the blue of a cloudless sky. Her flowers bloomed in abundant color, their red, yellow, purple, and white blossoms adding to the picturesque charm of her home.

For the past five years her heart had turned over in quiet anticipation each time she walked beneath the threshold of her wide oak doorways. But today, Bekka felt a different kind of anticipation. Today, the knowledge that Conor was there, in her home, filled her with a quiet urgency. He would soon be finished with the kitchen. And he would be gone.

Why did she feel this urgency to see him? Because, for five years, something had been missing from her life. Conor had stepped through her door and made her feel, made her come alive.

She followed her sons into the house, Jimmy carrying one sack of groceries, Jason huffing and puffing as he lugged two gallons of milk inside. Relieving her arms of the heavy sacks, she placed all their bundles on the dining room table.

The boys ran outside and she immediately searched for Conor. She'd expected to find him working inside, fastening oak trim around the doorways. The trim was nailed into place, but he was nowhere in sight.

Stashing the frozen grocery items inside the freezer, she closed the door, leaned her back against the refrigerator, and looked around. Since the kitchen was still unfinished, she left the other items on the table. Bekka ran her fingers over the rough cover of the library book and peeked out the window. Conor's truck was parked in the usual place, but he was nowhere near. She poked her head out the back door, but she didn't come into contact with his tall frame. The sandbox and swings were empty, too. Where was everyone?

She wasn't really worried; her sons knew their boundaries. She also knew kids didn't have to look far to find mischief and breathed a sigh of relief at the sound of Jason's voice, timid and far away.

She followed his voice around the side of the house, then wheeled back, out of everyone's view. Jason was perched on his bicycle, holding on for dear life. His training wheels had been removed and were leaning crookedly against one corner of the garage. "Don't let go," he pleaded. "Conor, don't let go . . ."

Jimmy said, "He can't do it, Conor. He's too scared. And he might fall."

Conor's voice held a soothing, reassuring quality, though she couldn't quite make out the words he spoke. Slowly, he began to walk, his right hand firmly grasping the bicycle's seat. Jason gradually began to pedal and Conor ran alongside at a steady gait down the length of the driveway.

Several times, when Jason froze in fear, Conor's strong hand steadied the small bicycle, his low voice quietly reassuring, encouraging Jason to keep pedaling. Up and down the driveway they went, Jimmy's cheers gradually replaced with silence.

Conor lifted his hand from the seat. Stretching his arm out in mid-air a few inches above the bike's back fender, he ran along next to the bicycle in case Jason needed his steadying hand. The look of concentration on Conor's face matched Jason's. Around and around the driveway they went, until Conor no longer needed to stabilize the boy at all.

Jason didn't know Conor had stopped beneath the shade of the oak tree, didn't know he was soloing. He didn't know Conor was watching, his hands on his hips, his feet firmly apart. The boy continued to pedal, his feet pumping up and down as he traveled the length of the driveway. A smile of wonder pulled at Bekka's mouth. She'd been trying to teach him to ride without his training wheels for months.

Jason navigated the turn and was headed back up the driveway when he noticed Conor standing in his path. Bekka laughed as he glanced behind him, as if he fully expected to see another Conor running by his side. He swerved, then steadied himself, a huge smile lighting his entire face. Everyone watched, Bekka, Conor, and Jimmy, and they all held their breath as Jason regained his balance.

"Mommy, look at me!" Jason called, the breeze lifting his straight hair away from his face.

She clapped her hands and laughed at his happiness. Conor turned, his eyes compelling her to meet his look. Hers gleamed with wide-eyed wonder, his smoldered with irresistible allure, and she knew she'd never forget a single detail of his face, would never forget a single detail of this moment.

Jason reached the patch of shade, braked, then jumped to the ground before his bicycle could tip over. "Conor! I did it! I really did it!" he shouted proudly.

Tears glistened on her lashes as she witnessed Jason's glory. She filled her lungs with fresh air, unaware of the silken smile that lingered on her lips. Conor encircled the small boy's waist and lifted him high into the air. Jason appeared weightless as he giggled with the pleasure of true accomplishment. His face alight with glee, a look of newfound adoration shone from his blue eyes. Conor dropped his head back and laughter rocked from somewhere deep within, combining with the higher pitched rejoicing of the boy he held in his large hands.

Before Conor lowered Jason to the ground, the child wrapped his arms about Conor's neck and hugged him tightly. The tenderness and trust in those arms, in the small heart beating against his own hard chest, made Conor's breath catch in his lungs. He closed his eyes, his hands resting upon the framework of each narrow rib.

The actual frailness of this small boy hit Conor with humbling clarity. He lowered Jason to the ground, his laughter replaced with misgivings. What if the child had fallen? Jason could have broken an arm or a leg or his neck . . .

Leave. Or else. That's what the note had said. Saturday night Conor had been convinced there was nothing anyone could do to hurt him. But the child he'd just held in his arms was another story.

What the hell did they mean? Leave. Or else. Or else, what?

"Jason! You rode your bicycle without the training wheels. And you did great!" There was no mistaking the joyful lilt in Bekka's voice as she knelt to hug her son.

Jason returned the hug. Pushing away, he bravely stated, "It was easy, Mom."

She gently clasped his chin in her hand. "Oh, it was, was it?" The boy grinned sheepishly up at her, having completely forgotten how afraid he'd been to even try it.

"Watch, Mom, I'll do it again!" With that he hopped onto his bike, and after an unstable beginning when his front tire wobbled precariously on the gravel, he steadied himself and rode away down the driveway.

He'd called her Mom. Jimmy had been calling her that for some time, but Jason always referred to her as Mommy. Until just now. Pride and love and the realization that time was passing moistened the sheen of her clear blue eyes.

She turned to the man responsible for Jason's fearless feat, her eyes glowing with wide-eyed gratitude. The eyes that met hers appeared nearly gray beneath the shade of the oak tree. There was a strange, indefinable emotion in his shadowed expression, his unreadable look stilling her splash of spontaneousness.

As she'd witnessed the man-child interaction between Conor and Jason, she'd been filled with an onrushing desire to be held in this man's strong arms. The spark of hope she'd carried in her heart all weekend quickly extinguished.

Bekka stopped herself short of sliding her arms around his waist and allowing the warm rush of tenderness she felt for him to flow. Instead, she stood perfectly still, one stride away from him, and simply said, "He is so proud. Thank you."

Conor released a long, audible breath. His gaze lingered on the glimmer of unshed tears in her eyes. She thanked him? Until this moment, he hadn't understood the enormity of his involvement with Bekka. He'd been aware of an intense physical attraction from the moment they met. In the days since, he'd come to desire her on another level, until his heart swelled with tenderness and a new emotion wove in and around his desire.

Love. He was falling in love, and he suddenly understood why *falling* was an apt word for the sensation. When you're falling, you aren't in control. He'd never been in love before. No wonder. How did anyone ever survive the fall? With Bekka, falling in love wasn't simple. Maybe falling in love never was.

She was everything he'd ever wanted in a woman, and more. She was beautiful and independent, strong and soft as only a woman could be. She was a wonderful mother and a true friend. She deserved the finest life had to offer, and he wanted to be the one to give it to her.

What the hell did that note mean? Who wanted him to leave? And why?

His life was nothing but problems, and she'd had more than her share already. He didn't know what was going on, didn't know why that lot was still in his name, didn't know who wanted him to leave, and he sure as hell didn't know why. But he did know she deserved better, better than unanswered questions, better than what he had to offer.

Bekka studied his serious expression. Only a moment had passed since she'd spoken, but an entire spectrum of emotions had cut across his face. She couldn't keep the faint tremor from her voice as she said, "Jason will never forget this day."

He swallowed hard, as if uncertain how to reply, as if he didn't want to be included in Jason's memory of this day, or as if he didn't feel worthy to be. When he recovered his voice, it still held a degree of uncertainty, and she felt an instant's squeezing hurt that he couldn't, or wouldn't, share whatever he was feeling with her.

Looking toward the horizon, he said, "I'd better get those new cabinets unloaded and moved into the house. Feels like it could rain."

She stepped into the sunshine and searched the horizon for signs of rain. The sky overhead was clear and blue, but dark clouds were gathering way to the north. Conor mumbled something about having a job to finish.

She watched until he rounded the corner and was out of sight behind the house.

Jason's expression was serious as he rode his bike up and down, concentrating on balancing without the help of training wheels. Jimmy wore a different serious expression, his chin touching his chest, aimlessly kicking a large pebble back and forth along the sidewalk beside the house.

"Jimmy, why don't you ride your bike with Jason?"

"Don't wanna."

"Would you like to play with your new truck in the sandbox?"

"Nope."

"Then how about coming inside with me?" she encouraged.

"Do I hafta?" he asked without looking at her, giving the stone another kick.

"No, honey, you don't have to. I just thought you might want to spend a little time with me." When he didn't reply, Bekka said, "Jimmy?"

He raised his head slowly, and she tried to read his look, but all he said was, "What?"

"What do you want to do?"

He looked back at the pebble near his shoe and, lowering his chin to his chest once again, said, "I'm going to kick this stone."

Trying to understand what had brought on this spurt of moodiness, Bekka walked past Jimmy and entered her home. Her thoughts wavered between Conor's moodiness and Jimmy's. What was wrong with those two?

Men!

SEVEN

The radio played softly from its perch on the back step. The familiar tunes of an old rock and roll song filled the air. Bekka didn't hum along with the lyrics. She didn't feel like singing. The radio covered the quiet but it didn't quiet her thoughts. She'd filled the wading pool for the boys and now sat near them as they played. Although she pretended to concentrate on her children, she was aware of every move Conor made.

She watched him load the saws and tools onto the bed of that old brown truck just as she had watched him often during the past two and a half weeks. But today his mouth wasn't shaped to a mellow whistle. He held his mouth in a straight line, as if he were deep in thought.

It was 4:31 in the afternoon. Bekka knew precisely because she looked from her watch to Conor as he finished loading the truck. He closed the tailgate with a noisy clank, then stood with his arms resting on its edge, his look focused somewhere on the faraway trees. His eyes narrowed in the bright sunshine, and his back became as straight as the boards he had nailed into place. She watched him, silently wondering what he was thinking.

He turned his head and his eyes met hers as if he had felt her gaze upon him. He squinted, the emotions lurking behind his eyes unreadable. She, too, squinted against the brightness, but her eyes didn't leave his face.

Conor took several long strides before stopping on the grass before her. "It's all finished?" she asked and wondered if he knew her question had a double meaning. At his nod, she said, "You're ahead of schedule, aren't you?"

"For a change, yes. When will the plumber hook up your sink?"

"Tomorrow. The linoleum will be put down the day after. Then Dad and Todd can move the refrigerator back into the kitchen."

Conor seemed more a stranger at this moment than he had the first moment they'd met. The thought came from a place beyond logic and reason. She didn't know what had happened to make him so distant. But something had, something between that tender kiss Saturday night and teaching Jason to ride his bike Monday morning. He cared for her, but something held him back.

She'd respect his privacy because Bekka, of all people, understood the right to one's own thoughts. Even though what she wanted to do was grasp his arms and demand that he look at her, somehow convince him he didn't have to be completely alone. Instead, she coated her voice with friendliness and said, "Looks like you're all packed up."

He was looking beyond her shoulder, through the windows to the newly completed kitchen. When his eyes met hers, he didn't hide the tenderness in his look. She touched his arm, her fingers a feather-light caress.

For his own reasons, Conor didn't feel he could confide in her, and she didn't know what to say to change his mind. So, instead of saying anything, she'd show him. Again. After all, a touch said more than words ever could.

She saw his eyes narrow on her mouth and knew he felt the gentle pull of her smile. Instead of turning away, Conor covered her hand with his, his thumb caressing her smooth skin. Bekka was entranced by the look and touch of him. She couldn't deny the spark of excitement that washed over her in the afternoon sunshine. Nor could she deny the sadness she felt that her time with him was ending. The birds tweeting in the trees, her children's noisy play, and the brightness of the sun dimmed as she took a step toward him and raised her face to his. His warm breath touched her cheek like a whisper. Her eyelids closed dreamily.

Instead of melting into his kiss, she felt cold water pelt her back and legs. Bekka's eyes flew open in surprise and she jerked away from Conor. She gasped as more splashes showered over her.

Jason shrieked, his devilish eyes glinting with mischief. Bekka and Conor darted away, outdistancing the new barrage of water. "Jason, you little . . ." The child laughed aloud as he darted off in the opposite direction.

Bekka's gaze settled on Jimmy, who stood outside the wading pool, silently watching Conor. In his eyes she saw so much uncertainty. A flicker of apprehension turned her look to one of worry. She went to him and, draping her arm across his bare shoulders, pulled him close to her side. He tilted his head, resting his blond curls against her ribs. Jason joined them, standing on her other side, his smile dimpling his heart-shaped face.

It was the image of Bekka standing between her young sons that Conor carried away with him, down the gravel road. She'd been about to kiss him, and his body hadn't fully recovered. He remembered her sigh, remembered her gasp when Jason splashed her with cold water. Most of all, he remembered the worry in her expression. That image didn't leave his mind as he drove to the house he was renting on the other side of town.

He'd been wise to clip the fragile ties drawing him to Bekka. His life was a mess, always had been. He hadn't paid Bud Trierweller to take care of that lot. He hadn't paid the taxes on it, either. Someone had. Now someone wanted him to leave. Conor didn't know who, or why. He only knew he didn't want to involve Bekka.

He'd been drawn to her smiles, had spent more hours than he cared to admit thinking about her. She was five feet five, a nice five feet five at that. She had honey-blond hair, a delicate nose, a stubborn chin, legs to die for, and breasts to ache for. But all women had hair and legs and breasts, and thoughts of them didn't keep him awake at night. He finally realized it wasn't her hair or her nose or even her breasts that made her so special. It was the way she made him feel, the way he felt when she was in his arms, the way she softened against him. It was wonderful. It was heaven, and it wasn't.

She accepted him. Without question, without judgment. She'd offered him friendship, and he knew they were on the brink of something deeper. But that note changed everything. It reminded him that his past wasn't really over.

Who put that note in his truck? Could Vince have done it? He was there at Bekka's party. But why would Vince want him to leave? It didn't make sense. Nothing made sense. It never had.

An hour later Conor kneaded the bunched muscles in his shoulder, no closer to an answer. It was stifling hot and his pacing wasn't helping him cool down, nor did it help relieve the knot in his stomach.

Wearing navy shorts and a sweatshirt, the sleeves cut off at the shoulders to allow for the muggy heat of the late June weather, he breathed deeply, raised his arms, and stretched the kinks from his legs. The blare of a horn invaded his concentration, and Mac Pearson pulled his gray company truck into the parking space next to Conor's Chevy.

"Hi, Conor ol' boy." Mac's loud voice thundered from his open window.

"Mac," Conor muttered.

"Did you get those blueprints I asked for?"

"They're on the seat of my truck."

Mac opened the door and retrieved the prints. A small sheet of paper came with the others. "What's this?" he asked, a flicker of apprehension narrowing his gaze.

"Something from my welcoming committee.'

"Do you know who it's from?" Mac glanced sharply around, his whole demeanor growing in severity.

"One person comes to mind."

"Vince Macelli?" When Conor didn't answer, Mac persisted. "Well?"

"I don't know, Mac. I just don't know." Conor wondered if his voice sounded as tired as he felt.

Neither said anything for several moments. "You told me all about that night you left town, about Vince Macelli's anger and that fire. Are you sure the fire was a result of faulty wiring and not intentionally set?"

"That's what the report said. That fire was thoroughly investigated, Mac, and it wasn't deliberately set. Bud Trierweller told me Leroy Macelli blamed me for that fire. God knows Leroy hated me, but for the life of me I don't know why. I was afraid of him when I was a kid, always steered clear of him, and he of me."

Conor stared at the ground as he continued. "Vince and I used to pretend we lived in the wilderness, far away from either of our fathers. We were both afraid of them, had both been on the receiving end of their tempers. Vince's father used to push Vince around, but he touched me only one time. Vince and I were twelve years old. We were playing stickball in Macelli's backyard and I hit the ball through a window. Leroy screamed that I was just like my old man, called me every name in the book, and shoved me off his property."

"Doesn't make much sense, a grown man treating a kid that way," Mac said. "But one thing's for sure, things are rarely what they seem."

Mac's statement eased the scowl from both their faces. Conor realized he wasn't really in this alone. He had Mac, and he might have a chance with Bekka. Hope and fear, desire and caution chased through his mind. It took him a moment to notice Mac was still talking.

"How are things going with the Stevenson woman?"

"You make it sound so simple."

"It is simple. Just like riding a bike. Once you learn, you never forget." Mac climbed into his truck and turned the key. One of Cher's songs pulsed over the radio. Conor had never cared for Cher. Maybe if she'd been blond.

"Hear that?" Mac called. "It *is* simple. It's in her kiss." He made the word *kiss* sound like pressurized air escaping a leaky valve.

Conor started to run in place, his end of the conversation spoken in short bursts. "Take your blueprints, Mac," he called.

"I'm going, I'm going. Just remember, problems have a way of working themselves out."

Mac drove away, and Conor began to run, his strides

long and even. *Not this problem*, he thought to himself. This problem had been lying idle for twelve years and seemed nowhere near the solving stage.

He was out of the parking lot, his strides carrying him effortlessly over the sun-baked pavement. As his shoes bounded across the cement and his lungs inhaled the warm, muggy air, his jumbled thoughts slowly began to clear.

It was 8:10. Conor had been gone exactly three hours and thirty-nine minutes. Bekka looked at the rays of the steadily lowering sun as they glinted through the windows of the completely remodeled kitchen, reflecting off the new counter and oak cabinets.

Okay. She admitted that she missed him, but she refused to give in to her dampened mood. After he'd driven away earlier that day, Bekka had looked around her, wondering what to do next. Instead of feeling remorse for something that obviously wasn't meant to be, she forced a spurt of ambition she didn't really feel and vigorously cleaned the entire house. She vacuumed and mopped and polished so that her home had never looked better. When she was through, the scent of fresh-cut lumber lingered, and Bekka realized it was going to take more than pine cleaner and a few hours to forget Conor Bradley's presence in her home.

She padded barefoot into the bathroom, her feet squishing on a discarded towel. Stooping, she picked up the heavy towel and wrung out the excess water over the bathtub. She exhaled a loud puff of air. Even with the windows open, the room was stifling. Leaves on the bushes outside the small window hung limp, waiting for the slight relief of a breeze that didn't blow.

She tidied the bathroom and wiped puddles from the floor. Jason and Jimmy had played in the large tub until the lukewarm water had turned cool. When they finally emerged, their fingers and toes were dimpled like raisins.

She stepped beneath the cool spray of the shower, the soft water washing over her heated skin. After patting her skin dry, she slipped her arms into the soft white material of an airy top and matching skirt. The fabric felt cool and light as it settled against her clean skin.

The boys were wearing only the bottoms of their pajamas, attempting to remain cool in the humid heat of the summer evening. Bekka took a tray that contained a pitcher of lemonade and ice-filled glasses out to the front porch. Jason followed with a bowl of grapes.

"Mom, is this right?" Jimmy asked, pointing to the beginner's model car he was painstakingly trying to put together.

"Let's see." Bekka studied the directions for a moment, then turned it upside down and studied it from that angle. She was a teacher, for heaven's sake. She'd excelled in college, was considered extremely bright by her colleagues. But when it came to deciding where figure D connects to figure E, she was lost.

She poured lemonade for each of them and took a sip of hers. "It seems right to me," she answered.

A shadow flickered across the grass. From the corner of her eye she caught a movement. Bekka stumbled to her feet, her heart lodged in her throat. The shadow moved steadily closer, and the directions in her hand crinkled and fluttered to the floor.

"Conor! You nearly scared me to death!"

His lips lifted in a semblance of a smile. "I seem to have that effect on people."

It was so easy to get lost in the way he looked at her, she felt trapped by her own emotions. "Are you thirsty?" The pitcher of lemonade sparkled on the tray.

"Have you noticed that you're always offering me something to drink?"

She didn't know what to say to that, so she simply nodded. She poured his drink and handed a glass to him. Conor took a sip, and while she poured more for herself, she felt her heartbeat flutter. He was standing on the ground, three steps down from her level. She turned her head, caught his gaze, and her smile deepened.

"Why are you here, Conor?" she asked quietly. "I didn't see any of your tools when I cleaned earlier."

She wanted to know what he'd forgotten. He hadn't forgotten anything, not a single detail of the past two and a half weeks, not her smile, not her scent, not her touch, certainly not her kiss.

Conor had to look away to hide his feelings. He pulled the front of his shirt out and wiped the sheen of perspiration from his face and neck. He was overheated from the high temperature and his long run. In comparison, Bekka looked as cool and enticing as a shaded lake. His gaze skimmed over the airy fabric covering her body, just as the material skimmed over her curves.

It was obvious she wore very little underneath, and his gaze lingered on the smooth swell of her breasts the light material covered but didn't hide. The muscles in his stomach contracted as another kind of heat invaded his body. He squared his jaw, fighting his own body for composure, and wondered if she was aware of what she did to him.

He considered telling her, but when his gaze traveled over her face, he couldn't reduce the moment to innuendos. She deserved an explanation, not cheap talk. "I wanted to explain. About this afternoon." That was honest enough.

Jimmy grew bored with his model, Jason with the adults' conversation. Taking the bowl of grapes, both children ran into the house. A minute later the sounds of their Friday evening television program blasted the air.

Bekka looked at Conor without moving, seemingly unaware of the captivating picture she made as she perched nonchalantly on the porch railing. She tipped her head to one side as she asked, "What did you want to explain?"

His eyes swept away from her, over the landscape, resting on the patch of garden in the side yard. "It sounds like the kids are occupied inside. If we stay out here long enough, we might stir up a breeze." If she didn't stop looking at him like that, she'd stir up a lot more.

They strolled across the wide yard, slowly making their way toward the garden. They talked about the weather. He told her about the plans he was drawing up for the house he'd build on his lot. She told him about the day she first saw her house in the distance. They talked about everything, except the heavy feelings between them, the feelings that had nothing to do with the muggy air.

"Technically, this garden belongs to Jason and Jimmy," she said from the garden's edge. "But I help them out with the hoeing and weeding."

Her voice worked over him, relaxing him by degrees, and, although it hadn't been a conscious decision, he knew why he'd come here. He came because he wanted to hear her voice, wanted to see her smile, and wanted her to understand.

They turned and started back toward the house. His voice, when it came, was as heavy as the air. "When I helped Jason learn to ride his bicycle, I had no idea how fragile he actually is. I've never been around little kids, never held one in my arms, until the other day when I held Jason. I actually felt his small heart beating.''

He turned his head, offering her his profile, the angles and planes of his tanned face tight with strain. ''His ribs aren't even as thick as my little finger. I practically forced him to ride his bike, and he could have been seriously hurt. I was on the receiving end of a belt or fist more times than I care to remember, but if Jason had fallen . . .''

He'd been worried about hurting Jason. That's why he'd stiffened, that's why he'd pulled away. Her heart ached for the childhood he'd had to endure, but she knew he wouldn't accept pity, so instead she offered him understanding. ''If he had fallen, he would have scraped his knee or skinned his elbow, but he would have healed. Conor, parents can't catch their children every time they fall. Just as we can't prevent them from falling. They're tougher than you think.'' Their inner hurts worried Bekka a hundred times more than scraped knees and mosquito bites.

They were walking side by side along the narrow sidewalk that connected the garage to the house. Leaning against the step was the book she'd found at the library two days ago, the book she'd chosen for Conor.

They both bent at the waist; her fingers grasped one corner, his the other. As she straightened, her breast brushed his upper arm. The sensation hardened her nipple and a passionate fluttering quickened her heartbeat. His smoky gaze touched her breasts, moving higher to her throat, finally resting on her face. Her breast still tingled from the brief contact, and she was sure a blush touched her cheeks.

She was becoming lost in the way he looked at her, so lost she bit her lip to keep from uttering his name. He released his hold on the book, his hands sliding up her arms, drawing her closer. He whispered her name, his breath hot and moist against her ear. She leaned into him, her hand gliding up his back. His swift intake of breath told her more than words ever could.

He kissed her thoroughly, and she responded by kissing him in return with sweet, shivery kisses. His lips moved over hers. His hands pressed her closer, his arms enfolding her in his embrace. Sliding one large palm over her back, Conor trailed his fingertips over her neck, then delved his fingers into her hair.

His lips left her mouth then, and his ragged breathing touched her ear as he feathered a kiss there. Bekka turned her head into his shoulder, and his musky scent filled her nostrils. Her eyes fluttered open, and she pressed her lips to his warm skin.

Her kiss was soft as dandelion fluff, her deep moan as erotic as moonlight on naked skin. The sound shook him. She shook him with so much feeling he ached. Sliding his hand from her silken hair, he brought his palm to her breast. Instinctively, she arched her body toward him, her breasts taut beneath his hand. She moaned again, and an answering groan escaped him.

Bekka's thoughts whirled as pleasure radiated from his touch. The blood rushing through her veins drummed in her ears, out of tune with the ringing coming from the house. She finally realized the sound wasn't her senses reeling, but the telephone. The fourth ring finally broke through her cloud of passion. She dragged her mouth from his. Laying her hand to his chest, she felt his heart throbbing beneath her palm.

Conor stiffened, loosening his hold on her, trying to regain his composure. Looking into her eyes, he took in a shuddering breath. It took every ounce of his willpower to keep from kissing her again.

"Mom, Uncle Mike needs you! . . . Mom?" Jimmy yelled loudly from inside.

"I'm coming," she called. She slipped from his

grasp and disappeared into her home. Conor closed his eyes, took several deep breaths, and followed the sound of her voice.

"Mom," Jimmy said, "Uncle Mike says it's real important."

"Okay, Jimmy." For Jimmy's sake she tried to keep the worry from her voice. "What's wrong, Mike?"

"Bek, Mara's still sick. I'm worried. She doubles over in pain and the pains are getting worse. Something's wrong and I'm taking her into Emergency."

"How long has she been like this?" Bekka asked.

"She's had pains for several days, ever since the volleyball party. She's hurting, Bekka." Normally cool, calm, and collected, Mike's voice was clipped with worry.

"Do you want me to come get your kids? They can spend the night here . . ."

"That's another thing. Missy came down with the chicken pox yesterday. And Marc's been so cranky and feverish. Your parents went to the lake. Could you come here?"

Conor watched her face from the doorway. Her questions were brief, the passionate blush on her cheeks replaced with worry. He could only hear her side of the conversation, but he surmised that Mara must be ill.

"Of course, Mike. I'll find someone to watch Jason and Jimmy and I'll be right there."

"I'll stay here with the boys, Bekka."

She turned, and when her eyes met his across the room, a thread of their earlier awareness resurfaced. His look was so galvanizing it sent her blood racing through her body.

Her mouth had gone dry, and her words, when they came, were spoken on a sigh. "Mike, I'll be there in five minutes."

Her brother-in-law didn't say good-bye, but before he hung up the phone, she heard him say, "Bekka's coming."

Bekka moved about her kitchen with speed and purpose. Taking her purse from the hall closet, she briefly explained the situation to Conor and Jimmy. Her footsteps quickly took her to the family room, where Jason was immersed in a television program. "Aunt Mara is sick and Uncle Mike's taking her to the doctor. I'm going to her house to watch your cousins. Conor will stay with you." Stooping, she planted a quick kiss on Jason's forehead, turned, and did the same to Jimmy's.

The boys stood there dazedly, and like a tornado, Bekka turned and skittered from the room. Conor caught up with her near the garage. He reached for her hand, stopping her for a moment. "Bekka, she'll be all right."

Her fingers trembled beneath his, and she squeezed his hand in return, trying to convey in her touch the tenderness she felt for him. She remembered the feel of his mouth, his heartbeat, his touch. The look in his eyes told her he did, too. Easing her fingers from his grasp, she turned and hurried to her car.

Conor dropped down to the step and opened the book Bekka had dropped there not more than ten minutes ago. "Is your mother going to do more remodeling?"

Jason pulled the book down toward his face. After studying the cover for a moment, he said, "That's the book Mom found for you, Conor."

"That was supposed to be a surprise, you dummy!" Jimmy scolded.

"Well, if it's 'sposed to be a surprise, why does Conor have it, then?" Jason rebuked.

Conor leafed through the illustrated book, marveling at the incredible relationship these two boys had. They could bicker like an old married couple, then run off to play as if nothing out of the ordinary had occurred. They were secure in the knowledge that they had each other. They were brothers, and he doubted they had any idea how lucky they were.

"See this picture?" He held up the photograph to the kids. "I worked on the house next door. See it there? Mac Pearson and I put those shingles on the roof ourselves."

Jimmy looked intently at the photograph, then leveled his eyes at Conor. "You lived in Detroit?" At Conor's nod, his gaze slid away and back again, along with his voice. "Our dad grew up in Boston."

"Is that where you lived before you moved here?"

"No," Jimmy replied, "I don't remember where we lived. Someplace in Ohio, I think."

Conor felt on the brink of understanding the boy and chose his words carefully. "Do you miss your dad, Jim?"

"Me and Jas don't miss him. We don't even remember him."

Conor could have argued with him. It was possible to miss something you couldn't remember, just as it was possible to miss something you never had.

"Do you have a dad?" Jason asked.

"No, Jason, but there's someone who's been like a father to me. His name is Mac, and if I could have chosen a father, I'd have chosen him."

"Do you have a brother?" the younger child asked.

"No. I had a friend . . ."

"Did he die, too?" Jimmy asked.

"No," Conor answered. But in a way, he had. Easing down to the next step, Conor pointed to another photograph. "See this house? I worked with the crew that remodeled it. It has seventeen rooms."

Jason sidled up close to Conor on the step, and

Jimmy tried to be unobtrusive as he inched his way closer for a better look. "If you don't have a dad and you don't have a brother, who do you do stuff with?" Jason asked.

He thought of Bekka and the *stuff* he wanted to do with her. His body hadn't completely cooled from their last *activity*, and thoughts like these weren't helping.

"Probably with Mac," Jimmy told his brother matter-of-factly.

Jason seemed to digest Jimmy's statement before asking, "Does Mac have any kids for us to play with?"

"Mac has two daughters, but I'm afraid Susan and Karen are all grown up."

"Susan and Karen?" Jason cried. "Their names don't even start with the same letter!"

Conor tipped his head to one side, grinning at Jason's logic. Jimmy tried not to laugh, but there was no disguising the amusement on his young face.

Jason's expression became serious. "Will Mom be gone long?"

"I don't know, Jas," Conor replied. "But don't worry, I'm going to stay until she gets back."

Jason laid his head on Conor's arm and whispered, "I wish you could stay forever."

The words sliced a chunk from Conor's heart, and he wished *forever* was a word he could contemplate.

EIGHT

Bekka had learned a long time ago to live with her sister's insuppressible straightforwardness, but she'd never seen her so pale, in so much pain. The living room looked like a sick bay. Missy lay at one end of the sofa, her face and arms littered with chicken pox. Mara lay at the other end, curled into a tight ball.

Bekka took the feverish baby from Mike the moment he entered the living room so that his arms would be free to help Mara to the car. "Have you given the kids anything for their fevers?"

Over his shoulder, Mike called, "An hour ago. All you can do now is keep them cool. There's some lotion somewhere . . ."

"Don't worry about the kids, Mar," she told her sister. To her brother-in-law, she whispered, "I can stay all night, if you need me, Mike. Just call me with any news."

Marc whined and Bekka ran her fingers through the baby-fine hair sticking to his forehead. Keep them cool? In this heat?

For the second time that day, Bekka filled a bathtub

135

with lukewarm water. She placed Missy and Marc in the tub and gradually added cold water to soothe their skin and lower their fevers.

Mindy kept up a constant chatter at her Aunt Bekka's side. "Mommy hurts. Maybe she had chicken pox in her tummy."

"I don't think so, Mindy. But the doctor will find out what's making her hurt. Your daddy and the people at the hospital will take good care of her."

She fed the children ice pops and fruit drinks, read them stories, then settled the girls into bed, a fan stirring the air in their room. Marc wasn't as easy to quiet. He didn't want to rock but relaxed when she walked, his head resting on her shoulder. The arm supporting her nephew went to sleep long before the baby did, but as she walked, his whimpering quieted. She moved through the quiet of another family's home, and thoughts of her own home swirled over her, thoughts of the man waiting for her there.

The house was strangely quiet. Jason and Jimmy were sleeping soundly in their bedroom upstairs. Even though she wasn't here, Conor felt Bekka's presence in every room, in every shadow. He'd given up pacing an hour ago, given up waiting for the phone to ring. Now he simply waited for Bekka.

From the front porch he gazed at the sky. The heavens appeared black, not a star in sight. Sudden gusts of wind stirred the leaves high in the trees. Crickets didn't chirrup, moths didn't flutter. A storm was brewing. He could sense it, could practically taste it. The coming storm heightened his anticipation of seeing Bekka, enhanced memories of her touch, her kisses, and her smiles.

It was midnight, and he wondered how much longer she'd be gone. He could stretch out on her sofa, but he knew trying to sleep was useless. He leaned against the porch railing, letting the cooler breeze wash over him. Glancing around, he noticed the pitcher of lemonade, glasses, and a plastic model car and all its parts scattered across the glass table.

Conor stacked everything on the tray and carried it into the house. He walked through the living room where curtains billowed as cool wind rushed in, chasing the muggy heat of the day out through the opposite windows. Placing the tray on the new counter in the kitchen, he took the back stairs two at a time and paused inside the first doorway.

Light from the hall slanted across the twin beds where Jimmy and Jason were sleeping. They looked small in their pajamas, small and innocent and secure. With careful movements Conor pulled a sheet over each of them, and they instantly snuggled into its softness. Their innocence drew him, touched him, in a way he'd never been touched before. They were innocent, yes, but far from perfect. They bickered and made messes and more noise than he'd ever imagined. But they were also sweet, and bright. They'd be easy to love. So easy.

Conor ran his hand through his hair, letting his breath out through pursed lips, then tucked the sheet beneath Jimmy's chin. He didn't know much about kids, less about tenderness. The kindnesses bestowed upon him hadn't come from his own parents, but from Vince's mother. Those kindnesses had made Vince's anger, his contempt, hurt all the more.

Conor stood in the doorway for several minutes, remembering another time, another place. He'd been a little older than Jimmy, closer to ten. His old man had been in one of his blackest tempers, so Conor had escaped to Vince's house, where he'd spent the night.

He'd heard the argument, heard Gloria Macelli's shouts and Leroy's curses, and had snuggled deeper into the lumpy mattress, trying to focus on the wind howling outside. A short time later the door had creaked open, and Vince's mother crept inside. When she covered them with another blanket, Conor pretended to be asleep. She lingered a moment over him, and when he'd opened his eyes, he was sure he saw tears glisten on her cheeks. He'd laid awake long after she'd tiptoed from the room, thinking about those tears.

He touched his forehead to the doorway and drew his thoughts to the present. He felt grubby all over from working and from his long, vigorous run. What he would have liked was a cool, cleansing shower. He wandered down the hall, looked into Bekka's bedroom, and continued on, not stopping until he reached the small bathroom at the end of the hall.

Bekka hadn't called, and he knew she could be gone for hours, possibly all night. Conor stripped off his clothes and stepped into the shower. He stood beneath that spray for a long time, turning his head and shoulders, letting the water wash over him. He lathered soap onto a washcloth and rubbed the day's grime from his body. Taking a plastic bottle of shampoo from the edge of the bathtub, he poured a portion of its contents into his palm. As he worked the shampoo into a lather, the scent of sweet apricots filled the shower cubicle.

He rinsed the shampoo from his hair, the lather sliding down his neck, over his back, and down his legs like foam. Turning the faucet off, he squeezed the water from his eyes and hair, then reached for a towel.

The first thing he noticed when he stepped from the shower was the wind howling through the eaves, rattling windows, and whirling over the roof. With the wind, the first raindrops pattered against the window panes. Conor pulled on his shorts, then ran to close the windows on the north and east sides of the house.

The wind had picked up, cooling his exposed skin,

whipping the curtains into his eyes. The last windows to close were in Bekka's room, and as he pushed the final one down, the faint light shining from the lamp on the bedside table wavered. He turned when the light flickered back on, and a movement near the doorway drew his attention.

Bekka watched Conor close the window. He was clad in nothing but the shorts he'd been wearing earlier, and the skin on his back appeared dark in the faint lamplight. She had to fight with the stubborn window each time she closed it, but not Conor. He barely had to apply added pressure and the window glided closed.

The lamp flickered out for a second, then caught, just as his gaze found hers. He stood, unmoving, the yellow rays of the lamp casting a warm glow over him. The look on his face caused her heart to trip in its beat. In all her life, Bekka couldn't remember any man ever looking at her with such intense longing.

Neither said a word, because words weren't necessary. A bolt of lightning flared across the sky, flashing through the window like a strobe light. As thunder shook the earth, the lamp flickered off again. This time it didn't waver back on.

More lightning and then another crack of thunder resounded through the quiet. Then there was nothing, no light, no human sound. The sudden darkness blinded him. Rain pelted the windowpanes, and wind howled through the eaves. A closet door squeaked as it was opened, and a moment later he first heard and then saw the light of a single match shiver through the darkness.

Bekka touched the match to the wick of a tall candle as lightning forked through the sky. The moment seemed suspended in time as they waited for the thunder. When it came, it was like a human pulse between them.

The candlelight threw shadows across her cheekbones, deepened the blue of her eyes. It illuminated the whiteness of her dress and clung to her smooth skin. In the faint light, the waving hair framing her face took on the richness of golden oak.

She saw tenderness in his gaze, and longing. Desire shimmered from him to her. The combination of those three emotions made her hand quiver and her heart flutter as she placed the candle on the stand near her bed. His gaze slid over her, slow and seductive. And when another streak of lightning bolted to the ground, her heart jolted, her pulse pounding.

With dreamlike steps, she went to him, her smile undoing the last thread of his self-control. Their fingers entwined, then slowly retreated. She slid her hands up his arms, over his bare shoulders. His arms encircled her and their lips met, the kiss slow, warm, and deep.

His hands explored every inch of her back, roaming from her waist to her shoulders, touching the softness of her hair a moment before traveling down again. She curled one arm around his waist, smoothing the corded muscles of his side, her palm traveling up his broad back and over the rolling muscles of his shoulders. Her other arm circled his neck, her fingers gliding through the damp tendrils of thick, dark hair.

His kiss was deep and urgent, and she kissed him in return with a hunger, an awareness that had lain dormant for a long time. She pressed her body closer and was suddenly lifted off her feet. He lowered her without ending the kiss, sliding her body down his body, man against woman.

The back of her legs brushed against the edge of her bed. Their lips parted, their eyes fluttered open. His eyes had turned a dark, stormy blue, and in their depths Bekka saw so many emotions. His desire flashed boldly. But she saw other emotions there as well.

He cared for her. She could see it, could feel it. It

was there in his barely restrained passion. He wanted her, in the most primitive way, but in another way, too.

Bekka felt the impact of the storm raging outdoors and the one spiraling in this very room. Her senses reeled as if short-circuited. She took his hand, kissed the corner of his mouth, his jaw, and his shoulder, then pulled him with her to the center of the soft bed.

Her skirt inched up her legs and his hand rubbed across her knee, upward, over the top of her thigh, outside and inside, and back again, each slow path taking his fingers higher than the last. A sigh rose from her at his touch. She'd never dreamed his hands, carpenter's hands, could be so gentle.

She pressed her palms to his chest. Conor eased her onto her back. He leaned over her, covering her breasts with his hard chest as he reclaimed her lips with a wildly swirling kiss.

Bekka arched her body into his as she ran her hands down the sides of his chest, along the border of his waist, and further across his lean hips. Her eyelashes fluttered against her cheeks, then up again when her fingers found what they'd been searching for.

His breathing became ragged, hers nearly stopped. The warmth emanating from him surrounded her in a cloud, where touch took the place of words, a sigh took the place of a promise, and kisses joined two lonesome hearts.

He eased his hand beneath her top, inching his fingers toward her breast. His lips whispered kisses along the column of her neck, nudged the buttons at her throat aside, trailing a warm path along the skin revealed there.

His hand covered her breast, and her nipple hardened in response to his intimate touch. As close at they were, he couldn't get close enough. His heart rate soared each time she moved against him, each time her hand glided over his skin.

His fingers brushed over soft fabric. He grasped the material in his hand, pulling it from the waistband of her skirt, and feared his heart might explode at the way she raised her arms, gracefully pulling the fabric up over her head in one fluid motion.

Lightning again illuminated the air. For a moment the room appeared as bright as day. In that moment, he memorized her, the softness of her smile, the column of her neck, the curve of her shoulders. As if someone pulled a chain, the brightness flicked off, throwing the room into near darkness once again.

Candlelight shimmered over her ivory breasts, and Conor followed the light, his palms covering her, his fingers kneading, caressing. She moaned as his lips brushed her nipples, her breasts heating as a dozen different sensations spiraled through her body.

Bekka lay back into the softness of the bed, her eyes closing, her fingers trailing into his damp hair as the scent of apricots wafted through the room. She slid her hand down the length of his body, not stopping until they encircled him, not stopping even then. This was a man whom Bekka trusted completely, her emotions running so deep she wondered if her heart would ever recover. Their remaining clothes were wisked away, and there were no barriers between them.

"I've dreamed of this." His deep voice was husky, his warm breath feathering her cheek, inflaming her desire.

Her whisper rivaled his for huskiness. "So have I."

Her words fueled his desire and he murmured her name, smothering her own sounds of pleasure with his next kiss. When he saw to protection, her heart swelled to the point of aching. As he covered her body with his, a new sensation filled her. Bekka clutched his shoulders as their bodies joined, gasping his name as they journeyed to that special place beyond the wind.

The storm raged on outside, the torrents cooling the heated earth as rain washed over the land. The air in the bedroom cooled, too. The subtle change in temperature sent a shiver down her body.

Conor felt her shiver. He pulled a lightweight quilt from its stand, covering them with softness. Bekka snuggled into his arms, a sigh escaping her lips. Neither spoke for several minutes, both lost in their own thoughts, listening to the wind and rain outside. His hand smoothed over her shoulder, hers splayed across his chest.

Bekka pressed a kiss to his shoulder before murmuring, "I hate the thought of going out in that rain to take you home."

"Are you trying to get rid of me?"

She raised her gaze to his, but the smile never made it to her lips. If she'd learned one thing about Conor Bradley, it was that actions spoke louder than words. So, instead of telling him, she'd show him. She'd tell him with her touch; she most certainly was not trying to get rid of him.

His gaze traveled over her face and settled on her eyes, the message in their depths as clear as the rain falling outside. Her heart quaked like thunder, swelling like a raging river.

Somewhere deep in his throat a moan resounded as her hand stole across his chest, down the center of his stomach. The degree to which he responded to her touch stunned her. But only for a moment, only for the moment it took for the flare of desire in his eyes to heat hers. He may have to work on accepting words, but he needed no tutoring when it came to accepting her touch. None whatsoever.

Sometime later reality resurfaced. She and Conor

were snuggled under a soft quilt. As far as she could tell, it was shortly before three in the morning, and a huge yawn overtook her. "Mmmmmm . . . I always knew I'd find a use for this quilt. Mara made it for me. She made one for nearly everyone. That was during her quilting phase."

"Her quilting phase?"

"For as long as I've known her, she's gone through one *helpful* phase after another. I remember when she first learned how to do macramé. She made macramé plant hangers and placemats for everyone. Then she took a ceramics class. And we all joked because for every occasion, be it birthdays, Christmas, the first day on a new job, anything, we'd receive a ceramic soap dish or flowerpot."

"Mara means well," Conor murmured against her hair. He also knew Mara didn't want her sister to become involved with him.

"She's probably the best sister in the world. And the pushiest."

"How is she, anyway?" When Conor had first seen Bekka standing in the doorway, his senses had been so filled with longing, he hadn't given a thought to Mara and her illness.

"The doctor removed her appendix, but she's going to be all right. Mike got back shortly after midnight. The poor guy was exhausted, but he said Mara's going to be fine."

"I'm glad," he said.

Conor's breath tickled her ear, and she turned her head to see his face. "Me, too. I told Mike I could stay all night to help with the kids, but he sent me home."

One corner of his mouth pulled upward. "Remind me to thank Mike."

"For what?"

"For sending you home. To me. I'm glad you came home tonight, Bekka." His voice had dropped to a sensuous plateau.

She held his gaze, and her voice was filled with truthfulness as she replied, "So am I."

She yawned again, snuggling under the quilt, trying not to fall asleep. "Jimmy and Jason can't find you in my bed in the morning. I'll have to wake them up to take you home."

His hand feathered a touch at her waist. "The couch will be fine."

"I can't let you sleep on my couch, not after you stayed with the kids."

Conor's hand made a slow journey up her side, skimming the edge of her breast, brushing over her shoulder and up her neck. Lowering his head to hers, he whispered, "I don't mind. Really." His body was already beginning to tighten. Again. He doubted he'd get much sleep no matter where he slept.

His mouth claimed hers, and his heartbeat quickened. Passion mounted in his body. Reluctantly, Conor pulled away from her, wishing he'd brought more protection. If he stayed where he was, within touching distance, he'd be tempted to say to hell with protection. It took incredible self-control to pull himself away from her, but he refused to take such a chance. He wouldn't hurt her, not in a million years.

He scooped his shorts from the floor and pulled them on while Bekka slipped her arms into a floor-length robe. The raging storm outdoors had quieted to a steady rain, just as the one in this very room had quieted.

The lamp had burst on earlier, but at the time their eyes had been closed, their senses elsewhere, and neither had noticed. Placing her hand behind the flame, Bekka bent and blew out the candle. As she took fresh sheets and a pillow from the hall closet she noticed her muscles suffered from an intense languidness. She smiled as she remembered what had caused it.

Flipping on light switches along the way, she led Conor to the sofa in her family room, where she shook out the sheet and tucked it into the cushions. Fluffing his pillow, she said, "Are you sure you'll be all right here?"

"I'll be fine." He hugged her tight to his body, letting her know how *fine* he could be again.

She breathed in the scent of apricots and exhaled on a sigh. "Mmmm. Your hair smells good. Like apricots."

In a deep whisper, he said, "It was the only shampoo I could find."

She slipped from his grasp and started up the stairs while he stretched his body out on her sofa. His feet knocked against the armrest at one end, and his head bumped against the other. He heard her whisper, "Good night, Conor," as she drifted up the open staircase.

She probably had no idea the thin ivory-colored robe became translucent in the darkness. He stared, wide eyed, up at the ceiling. His body was still reacting to her scent, to her voice, to the outline of her body beneath that robe.

It was apt to be a long night—by far the longest and the best night of his life. As he lay there listening to night sounds in the country, he thought about Bekka and her two little boys. And he smiled.

Bekka stretched her body, marveling at the comfort of her warm bed. Drifting between the deep sea of sleep and the wide sky of wakefulness felt wonderful. She tried to move her leg sideways, but something, some weight, restricted her movement. With her eyes still closed, she rolled to her side.

Beneath her lowered eyelids, she could see bright

sunshine irradiating the morning. She finally forced her eyes open and found blue eyes so like her own staring back at her from a distance of no more than six inches.

"Hi, Mom," Jason whispered.

"Hi, yourself," Bekka whispered in return. When she rolled to her back, she felt the tug of blankets on the other side of her bed. Jimmy was perched there, opposite his younger brother.

"Good morning!" she said brightly.

"Shhh!" Jimmy quieted her.

"Why are we whispering?" Bekka asked her sons, lowering her voice to match their whispers.

"Cuz Conor is sleepin' on the sofa downstairs," Jason explained.

Pulling her arms winsomely above her head, she stretched, being careful to keep the blanket around her neck. Normally, she slept in a knee-skimming nightgown, but somehow, after leaving Conor on the sofa downstairs last night, she couldn't bring herself to don her gown. She'd crawled beneath the sheets wearing nothing at all.

"Why is he still here?" Jimmy asked petulantly.

"Conor ran out here, and when I got back from Aunt Mara's, a thunderstorm had blown in. So, rather than wake you boys up, Conor slept on the sofa." She thought about everything she and Conor had done *before* she'd led him to the sofa and was thankful the boys were too young to interpret the warm blush on her cheeks.

"What's wrong with her?" Jimmy asked.

"Who?"

He exhaled a loud puff of air that seemed to say "Who do you think? Aunt Mara."

Oh, her. Bekka hid a smile to herself. Something seemed to have happened to her mind. What had Conor done to her to make her feel so marvelous? She knew.

The memory was imprinted on her mind as well as in the most tender areas of her body.

She realized that what she really needed was time alone with her thoughts. What had happened between them last night hadn't been planned, but she felt it had somehow been inevitable. She was in no way sorry it had happened.

What did Jimmy ask you? Oh, yes, Mara.

"Aunt Mara had surgery last night. The doctor removed her appendix, and although she'll be sore for a few weeks, she's going to be fine. You should see Missy and Marc. They have the chicken pox."

"What's a 'pendix and what are chicken pots?" Jason asked.

Bekka ruffled Jason's straight hair and laughed. "An appendix is a small tube inside our bodies attached to our intestines. And chicken pox is a disease that usually children get. It makes them itchy and cranky."

"If children get it, why don't they call it children pox?" Jimmy asked logically.

She smoothed a curl from Jimmy's forehead and, ruffling his sleep-messed tendrils, murmured, "That's a good question."

She sent the boys back to their room to dress before gingerly sliding her feet to the floor. Her eyes caught her reflection in the full-length mirror, and as she turned this way and that, she was surprised to see nothing had changed. Outwardly she was the same.

One thing certain in this life is that you cannot undo something that had been done. She'd sworn she'd never become involved like this again, would never allow heartache to touch her heart again. Last night her body and her heart became entangled with Conor's. She didn't want to undo it, not a single moment. She'd wanted to give him friendship and had ended up giving him a lot more than that. How could she be sorry for the most wonderful night of her life?

Heavy drawers opened and closed down the hall as her sons dressed for the day. She, too, began to dress. Last night's thunderstorm had lowered the temperature. Bekka pulled on pants for the first time in weeks, then poked her head and arms through the openings of a summer sweater.

After sliding her feet into shoes, she smoothed the wrinkles from the floral-patterned sheet, memories of last night washing over her. She remembered their bodies as they moved gracefully through the dreamlike haze of candlelight. She'd nearly forgotten who she was. Her nerve endings had dropped straight to her toes, and she still hadn't recovered. She was in love.

Jason was haphazardly pulling his blankets up in the pretense of making his bed. Jimmy's was so messed, the covers so tangled, the sheet pulled completely out, he gave up and let Bekka finish it for him. "Jimmy," she asked, "are you having bad dreams? Is that why your sheets are pulled out?"

"I don't think so," he answered. "I don't remember any bad dreams. Maybe I'm getting too big for this bed."

Bekka ruffled his hair and smiled. "You're getting big all right, but you haven't grown out of this twin bed yet."

In the bathroom she splashed warm water on her face, then brushed the tangles from her hair before securing it at her nape with an ivory barrette. She brushed her teeth and applied mascara to her lashes and gloss to her lips, then went down the back stairs with her sons. The kids tiptoed dramatically to the family room and brought back minute by minute reports that Conor still slept. Just thinking about seeing him brought a smile to her lips.

The boys were as busy as two buzzing bees as they placed a mixing bowl and milk, flour, and bacon on the dining room table. As far as they were concerned, nothing had changed. It was Saturday morning and every Saturday morning they helped prepare a big breakfast.

She poured water into the coffee maker while Jimmy stirred the juice. She whipped up pancake batter while Jason set the table, just as they did every other Saturday morning. The morning wasn't different. She was.

Conor awoke to the delicious aroma of fresh coffee brewing and the sizzling sound of frying bacon. He made his way to the bathroom, where he shrugged into his shirt. He buried his face in a warm washcloth and slowly rubbed his hand across the sandpaper roughness of his chin.

He could have used a shave, but what he really wanted was to pull Bekka into his arms and feel her body tremble as she melted into him. Just thinking about it sent a new wave of desire strumming through him.

He never thought he'd have it all. Not when he was a kid, certainly not when he'd come back to Millerton. The most he'd hoped for was a decent life, a thriving business, an honest reputation. Last night he'd found more, more than he'd dared dream. For over two weeks he'd glimpsed bits of her tenderness, her caring, her stubbornness. But last night she'd given him everything, brashly handed him her innermost feelings. She'd trusted him with her body, and Conor was amazed at the extent of his feelings.

Maybe he could have it all. Maybe he could have Bekka, share her life, share her children. Maybe there was still a chance for the kid from the wrong side of the tracks.

Her informants notified her that he was up moments

before he entered the dining room. As she looked from the hot plate, where she was flipping pancakes, to his face, she was aware once again of that simmering attraction she'd felt from the first moment they met.

His dark hair was neatly combed. The early morning shadow of his unshaven face looked the tiniest bit undignified. His eyes wore an expression of intimacy, and his voice held the dawning depth of the new day as he said, "Good morning."

"Good morning. Would you join us for breakfast?"

He would have liked to join her for a lot more. He nodded, and Jason took his hand, leading him to the table where four places were set. "You can sit here, Conor. It's almost ready."

He sat, when what he wanted to do was take her in his arms. He wanted to hold her close. Jim and Jas filled the silence with small talk, and Conor answered when an answer was expected. But he was aware of her every move.

"The plumber is coming in a little while," she said. "Just think, two more days and I'll be able to fix breakfast in my new kitchen."

Her hips swayed beneath the body-hugging fabric of her slacks, and Conor knew precisely how smooth her flesh had been beneath his fingers. The soft weave of her sweater covered her slender curves. But Conor knew the delicious softness hidden underneath, knew the skin there would be infinitely smooth and paler than the sand color of her sweater.

"Bekka, did you sleep well?" he asked with deceptive calm.

She was flipping pancakes onto the platter, and at his question her look settled to his across the narrow room. Her voice was shakier than she would have liked, but she answered truthfully. "I slept wonderfully. And you?"

"Undeniably the best I've ever had."

Their conversation went right over the top of the boys' heads, and the double meaning of his reply sent a ripple of awareness over her body. The hidden message in his voice echoed her own longings.

The bacon spattered. Bekka jumped when it hissed and popped, turning her attention from Conor to the task of preparing breakfast. There was a tingling in her empty stomach, and she had to fight her overwhelming desire to go to him, to glide her hands around his neck and over his broad shoulders.

She caught him looking her over seductively while they ate their meal. She buttered the kids' toast and sipped her coffee, listening with only one ear as Conor told the boys about the new forklift trucks he'd ordered for the company. He sent her a knowing look, and she stared at him longingly over the rim of her steaming mug.

Jason and Jimmy fled to the family room the moment they were finished. Bekka met Conor's gaze across the littered table. "I can let these dishes soak if you're in a hurry to . . ."

Her words trailed away at the look in his eyes, at the way he pressed his hands to the table and slowly stood. The next thing she knew he'd rounded the table. She didn't remember having stood up but knew she must have. His arms came around her and his lips found hers. His hands explored the soft lines of her back, waist, and hips.

Everything seemed brighter today, as if last night's rain had cleansed the entire world. The air was comfortably cool, his arms bracing. She kissed him, and with a pulse-pounding certainty, she knew his feelings for her ran deep.

His lips left hers, and his words tickled her ear. "I've wanted to do that since the moment I opened my eyes."

She touched her forehead to his chin, then turned her head into his shoulder, reveling in the feel of the man in her arms. "Oh, Conor, I think I could stay like this forever."

For a moment he contemplated forever, forever with the woman in his arms, forever with the children in the next room . . .

Noise split the quiet. Shattering glass exploded, clashing through the air, crashing to the floor.

"Mommy!"

Bekka's heart lodged in her throat. She raced to the family room, fear and dread slicing through her. Every mother alive knew the sound of her child in pain.

NINE

Both boys were crying. Both were bleeding.

"Don't move!" Bekka commanded. Her smooth-soled shoes crunched over shards of glass in her hurry to reach her children.

"Mom, it's in my hair," Jimmy sputtered.

"Don't touch it," she murmured. "I'll get it out of your hair. Shh. You're all right. Mommy's here."

"I'm b-b-b-bleeding," Jason wailed.

"Here, Jason, let me see. There, there," she crooned. "It's not deep. Just a little scratch."

She picked shards of glass from their hair, examined their arms and faces, the tears springing to her eyes a delayed reaction to her fear. "What happened?"

Jimmy answered, "I was putting my model together. The window broke and glass flew everywhere."

"How did the window break?"

The boys were calmer now, but her thoughts were still jumbled in confusion. Bekka's gaze darted from the floor littered with glass to the pieces that had fallen to the windowsill before turning to look at Conor.

It took several seconds for her eyes to adjust to the

change in him. He stood near the window, surrounded by pieces of glass. In his hand he clutched a brick. Tied to the brick was a sheet of paper. She stiffened as she realized what had happened.

"Someone threw a brick through the window?"

At his nod, ice seeped into every pore. She shivered and knew it had nothing to do with the drop in temperature. For a moment hurt and longing lay open in his eyes. Then his expression clouded, and his lids slipped down. When he reopened them, the longing was gone.

"Who?" she asked.

"It doesn't say."

He'd withdrawn, and the realization was as sharp as the jagged pieces of glass in her hand. She placed the glass on the table and tenderly took her sons' hands. She led them to the bathroom, where she cleaned their scratches and applied ointment and Band-Aids.

"Did someone throw that brick on purpose?" Jason asked.

"Of course they threw it on purpose," Jimmy taunted. "Nobody would throw a brick with a note on it by accident."

"Who, Mommy?" Jason asked, his blue eyes wet with tears.

"I don't know, sweetheart," she replied. "But don't worry, I'll find out." She took extra care combing through their hair, searching for tiny shards of glass. When she was completely satisfied that none were left, she dropped to her knees and hugged them both.

She instructed the boys to stay clear of any glass, then hurried back to the family room, where Conor was bent over, close to the floor. He'd already stacked the larger pieces of glass in a pile and was picking smaller shards from the carpet. His palm was full, his expression, when he turned her way, was guarded. "Are they all right?"

Bekka nodded. She didn't know how to penetrate the deliberate blankness in his eyes. She held a wastebasket in one hand and grasped his wrist with the other. Glass tinkled to the bottom of the basket as she carefully tipped his hand over.

"You're cut," she murmured.

"It's nothing."

It wasn't nothing. Something in his manner, in his expression, a flicker deep in his eyes, made her increasingly uneasy. She let go of his wrist and helped clean up the remaining pieces of glass.

"What did the note say?" She watched him intently. Instead of answering, he shoved the paper into her hand.

Leave. Or burn.

She gasped but tried to maintain an outward calm. "Conor, what's going on?"

"The last one said 'Leave or else.' Bekka, I never wanted to involve you in this."

Her gaze was drawn to his hand. As if unaware of the glass in his palm, he drew his hand into a fist. Pain etched his face. She took his hand in hers and watched as he uncurled his fingers. Beads of blood rose from his calluses, and Bekka took the shard of glass from his palm.

Even the tough could bleed, even the callused hands of a carpenter. She tucked the thought away. "This isn't the first note?"

He shook his head, and Bekka realized he'd faced the other note alone. She wondered what it would take to convince this man he wasn't alone anymore.

"I think we should call the police."

He reacted to the concern in her voice and cursed himself for allowing her to get involved in this mess. Conor's gut felt like a cave, a cave filled with bitter, cold despair. He'd been afraid Jason would be hurt learning to ride his bicycle. He now realized how insignificant that had been and cursed himself for allowing real danger to touch Bekka and the boys, cursed the loneliness in his soul.

"Are you sure the boys are all right?" He could hear them talking in the kitchen, talking about shattered windows and bricks and bad guys.

"They're okay, Conor. Really."

"I shouldn't have been here this morning. If I hadn't been, they wouldn't have been hurt."

Conor watched her weigh the brick in her right hand with the same deliberateness she seemed to be weighing her next words. "Don't blame yourself for another person's actions. You didn't throw this brick. Let's find out who did and put this to rest once and for all." She'd used her most authoritative teacher's voice for the first sentence, but the rest was spoken with depth, with the intensity of a person feeling his pain.

She went to call the police, and Conor watched her go. She wanted to help him, but she didn't know the risk she was taking, the risk to her safety and to Jimmy and Jason's. He'd do whatever it took to keep them from harm, even if it meant severing all ties to Bekka and her sons.

Two policemen arrived, Vince Macelli and a younger man named Adam Miller, who was no relation to Mike. Vince took down the pertinent information, and Bekka was amazed to learn that today was Conor's birthday. That brick had been some gift.

She knew the exact moment Vince noticed the breakfast dishes on the dining room table, knew the exact moment he noted the fourth place setting and the exact moment he understood the implications. He cast no judgment, and for a split second she saw an incredible similarity to Conor.

"Were you out on a call twenty minutes ago?" Conor asked the other man.

She watched them stare each other down, not certain how to anticipate Vince's reaction to the ominous question. She wondered if Conor really believed Vince was capable of throwing that brick and waited in silence for Vince's reply.

It was the other officer who answered. "We were at the station, filling out those god-awful reports."

"You were together?" Conor asked the younger man.

"Yeah, why?" he replied.

Vince was aware of the implication. It was there in his eyes, in his voice. Bekka felt a glimmer of admiration when he didn't give in to Conor's provocation. Instead, he asked, "Do you have any idea who might have thrown that brick?"

"No. Do you?" Conor's voice was as low as it could get, deep and controlled.

Vince quirked his eyebrows, Conor drew his downward, and Bekka held her breath. When Vince didn't answer, Conor ran his hand through his hair, down over his unshaven face. "I'd appreciate it if you kept this quiet."

Vince nodded, then both police officers left. Watching them go, she couldn't shake the feeling Conor wanted to say something to Vince and Vince to Conor.

Bekka knew Jimmy and Jason were worried when they began stacking dishes without being told. With a soft pat to each of their behinds, she said, "I'll do these dishes, boys. Why don't you two run on outside and play."

"Goody!" Jason piped, turning immediately toward the door. "Come on, Jimmy, let's ride our bikes."

"Stay in the yard," she called. "And don't go too close to the road."

"Do you think the person who threw that brick will come back?" Jimmy asked.

"I don't think so, honey. I don't think that brick was meant for us."

"You think it was meant for Conor?"

Bekka nodded, and Jimmy followed Jason out the door, but not before she caught him casting a long glance from her to Conor and back again.

The door slammed shut behind the boys, and she turned to Conor, who was inspecting the damage to the window. "This is double-plated glass. The entire window will need to be replaced. I'm pretty sure we have one in stock."

"Conor," she whispered.

He finally looked at her, his expression as jagged and painful as the broken glass. As casually as she could manage, she said, "You don't have to do that. I can call the glass place north of town."

"I'll do it."

"Why?"

"Because I feel responsible, dammit."

She exhaled all her breath on a slow sigh. "Then what you're feeling is misplaced responsibility. You didn't throw this brick." She turned it over, moving it from one hand to the other.

"I said I'll fix it."

"Fine. Just so you know you're fixing it because you're my friend, not because any of this is your fault."

Friends? Last night they'd gone past friendship, way past. Last night she'd given something to him she'd never given to anyone, not even Ted. She'd given Ted her heart, but she felt as if she'd given Conor a piece of her very soul.

Their lovemaking had been like a bridge uniting them. Now she felt as if they stood on opposite banks of a river, and Conor was acting as if the brick that had burst through her window had blown their bridge right out of the water.

Bekka knew she hadn't given her heart lightly, just as she knew bridges weren't the only means to cross a river. She'd find another way, a stepping-stone into his heart. Being careful not to touch him anywhere else, she stretched up on tiptoe and gave him a quick kiss. It was nothing like their previous kisses, just a feather-light touch of her lips on his beard-roughened chin.

He didn't move, not a muscle. But she heard his quick intake of breath and knew he was affected. A war silently raged inside him, and whether he knew it or not, he wasn't fighting it alone.

Conor felt that burning sensation in the pit of his stomach again. Frustration. He tensed his jaw, his lips thinning to a straight line. She wasn't making it easy to turn away, but it was the only way he knew to keep her safe.

Being this close to her was testing his patience, like sore muscles that ached after a strenuous uphill run. If he didn't put some distance between them, he feared he'd give in to the temptation to kiss her, to say to hell with being alone. His eyes narrowed on her mouth, and he might have lowered his lips to hers . . .

The knock on the front door brought reason back to his brain. He swore under his breath and scowled. It was almost impossible to kiss this woman without interruption. Phones had a way of ringing, children had a way of splashing them, people had a way of knocking on the doors at the damnedest times. He should have thanked each one for the interruption. He felt like cursing them all.

She opened the door to the plumber, who marched past them both with a grumble about doorbells that didn't work. He stopped and blew a toothy whistle at the broken window. "The kids put a ball through that glass?"

"Something like that," Bekka answered without looking at Conor.

The plumber ambled past them both, his toolbox clanking to the floor in the kitchen. Conor didn't say another word. He cast one last look at the broken window and walked out the door, over the front porch, and down the steps.

"I'd be more than happy to give you a ride into town, Conor," she called to his back.

He stopped and slowly looked back at her. "The exercise will be good for me." Without another word, he turned around and began to run.

Bekka stood in the doorway and watched as he lengthened his stride, dodging water puddles in her driveway. He wasn't walking away from this battle, she thought wryly. He was running. She was pretty sure he'd tried to keep the feeling from his voice, from his eyes, but she knew, even if he didn't, that they weren't through. He'd be back, to fix the window. For now, that was enough.

She stood in that doorway for a long time, staring into the distance where Conor was no longer visible. Last night, in his arms she had discovered a new dimension of sexuality she hadn't known she was capable of feeling. This morning he was trying to protect her from harm, but she didn't believe, not for a minute, that he'd forgotten what they'd shared.

Song sparrows splashed playfully as they bathed in the water puddling her driveway. She folded her arms close to her heart and was lost in her own introspective contemplation. One question drew her thoughts back to earth: How had the person who'd thrown that brick known Conor was here?

She looked from the brick in her hand to the quilt

and pillow nestled on the sofa where he had slept. *Who could have thrown that brick? Who knew Conor was here?* There weren't a lot of choices, but something didn't add up.

She placed the brick on the table, shook the wrinkles from the quilt, and folded it neatly. Placing the pillow on top, she carried the bundle up the open staircase. The pillow's center was indented where Conor's head had rested throughout the night. Sitting on the edge of her bed, she touched the tip of her nose to the imprint, and the scent of apricots filled her nostrils. Memories washed over her, memories of last night, memories of her newly awakened love.

Conor's feet rebounded across the gravel road. Another mile to go. The burning frustration in his stomach had diminished to cold ashes. Running always eased the knot of tension from his body. He wondered what it would take to relieve the cold feeling that had dropped like lead when he'd read that note.

Leave. Or burn.

He'd wondered what the 'or else' in the last note had meant. Now he knew. Knowing didn't make what he had to do any easier.

As Conor ran, memories of Bekka filled his mind and body with new-felt longing. She'd gotten to him as no other woman ever had before. He increased his steady pace, a thought jangling through him with every stride. Few people knew he'd spent the night at Bekka's. He could think of only four. He and Bekka, Jimmy and Jason. Who threw that brick? How in the hell had that person known he was there?

He increased his speed, as if being chased by a demon.

It was nearly dark outside by the time he finished replacing the window. Mac hadn't had one in stock after all, and Conor had driven to Lansing, scouting three different window companies before he'd found an exact match. He unhooked his tool belt and stepped back to survey his work.

Lamplight glowed from one corner of the room. Bekka had turned it on twenty minutes ago, then spun round without a word and headed back into the kitchen. He could hear her voice from here, talking to Jim and Jas, answering questions, laughing.

Conor glanced around the room, at the comfortable furnishings, the soft lamplight, and the family photos grouped on one wall. He remembered the first night he'd studied her pictures. He'd barely known her then, barely knew her smile, the twinkle in her eyes, her sighs, and her passion.

Her laughter carried from the kitchen to his ears. That voice, that deep, sultry voice. It drew him. She drew him.

From the corner of his eye he caught a movement in the archway. Jim and Jas watched him, a curious expression on their faces. He wondered what they were up to.

"Conor," Jason crowed. "Come here. I have something for you in the kitchen."

"What is it, Jas?" he asked.

"You'll see," Jim answered. Without waiting for his next question, the kids turned and ran back to the kitchen, back to their mother. He had no choice but to follow.

Before he reached the kitchen, the light went out and candlelight lit the room. "Surprise!" three voices called in unison, two childishly high and one sultry and deep.

Jason flicked the light back on, and they all squinted at the sudden brightness. "Mommy told us today's your birthday. Happy birthday, Conor!"

A lump formed in his throat, then slowly slid down to his stomach. The woman was playing dirty.

"Come on, Conor," Jim sputtered. "Make a wish and blow out your candles."

He stepped up to the counter he'd built only days ago. "Close your eyes and make a wish," Jason ordered. "If you wish real, real hard, it might come true."

He closed his eyes and wished with all his might. When he opened them, his look collided with Bekka's. He took a deep breath and blew out every last candle.

"What was your wish?" Jason asked.

"He can't tell us, you dummy," Jim admonished, "or it won't come true."

"Oh, yeah," Jason replied. "I forgot."

Bekka saw the tenderness in Jimmy's expression when he looked into Jason's face, and her own heart swelled with pride for all three of these special people, her sons and the man she loved.

"Hurry, Mommy," Jason piped. "Me and Jimmy are starving."

She ruffled his smooth hair and replied, "You and Jim are always starving. Especially when there's cake and ice cream to eat."

She took plates from the shelf. Holding the door open, she said, "Look at this. I have a kitchen again." She ran water in the sink. "And running water. All the modern conveniences of the twentieth century." But she didn't have him. Heaviness centered in her chest. He'd come back to fix the window. But he wasn't really here. It was as if he'd left a part of himself behind, the part he'd given to her last night. She wanted that part back. She wanted him, all of him.

She'd cleaned up every last speck of glass this morning and spent the entire afternoon organizing her new kitchen and organizing her thoughts. Glasses were in the first cupboard to the right of the sink, plates to the left. Pots and pans were near the stove, towels in the island, along with placemats and plastic ware. Organizing the kitchen had been simple. Figuring out what to do about Conor was not.

Jimmy and Jason seemed to have recovered from their fear of having that brick sail through the window. Their Band-Aids had come off by late afternoon, and although Jason had reverted to calling her Mommy, neither child seemed to have any lasting effects from the scare. Conor was another story.

The boys plucked the candles from the cake, counting them one by one. *One, two, three* . . . She found as many reasons to love Conor as there were candles on his cake. He was strong and ambitious and caring.

Four, five, six. Proud, self-sufficient, and honest . . .

Thirteen, fourteen, fifteen . . . Hard-working, tender-hearted, and trustworthy. He was noble, unselfish, and possibly the most stubborn man she'd ever met, which was saying a lot since she herself came from a long line of stubborn people.

Twenty-six, twenty-seven, twenty-eight. He could make her swoon with one kiss, make her come apart in his arms.

Twenty-nine, thirty. He was the man she loved, plain and simple.

"Thirty years old?" Jason asked. "Wow!"

Bekka cut the cake. "The birthday boy gets the first piece," she declared, handing a plate to him.

"Mom didn't know what kind of cake you liked. She made spice, cuz she says everybody likes spice," Jimmy stated.

She studied the brooding man from across the counter. She knew precisely how the muscles in his stomach contracted when she ran her palm down its center, knew the sound he made when she held him in both her hands. She knew how he felt, how he made her feel in return. She knew all those things, but she didn't know what kind of cake he preferred. And she didn't know how to convince him she believed in him.

Bekka was so carried away by her thoughts, by the way his gaze moved over her face and her shoulders, dropping to her breasts, she failed to hear Jimmy the first time he spoke. "Are we going to have ice cream with our cake?" he repeated.

"What? Oh, of course." She hurried into the dining room to get the ice cream, aware that the magnetism that had built between her and Conor these past weeks hadn't diminished. In fact, it was growing stronger.

"Just think," she murmured as she bustled from cupboard to drawer. "In two more days the refrigerator will be back in the kitchen where it belongs." She dished up the ice cream and wondered how long it would be before Conor accepted her love. Biting her lip, she wondered what she'd do if he never did.

The kids finished their cake and ice cream, then ran off to play before bedtime. Bekka filled the sink with water and vigorously began washing the plates and forks. For the first time since they'd met, she didn't know what to say to him. "I could have used the dishwasher, but it seems so good to have running water . . ." Her voice trailed off into thin air.

Conor leaned one hip against the counter. As he watched her hurried motions, his mind turned to last night, and he felt trapped by his own emotions. He wanted her. And she was here, so close. He plunged his hand into the water with the intention of stilling her movements. He covered her fingers with his own and raised her hand with his, suds dripping from their entwined fingers.

The look of desire in her eyes hypnotized him so that he wasn't even aware his thumb stroked back and forth across her palm. Desire. He's seen it in her eyes last night, heard it in her sigh. But this morning when that brick had shattered her window, when shards of glass has flown through the air, when her children could have been seriously injured, he'd expected her to turn away, to blame him. She hadn't, and she didn't. But she should. For her own good, she should.

She picked up a sunny yellow towel and blotted the suds from their wet hands. Mere inches separated their bodies. Last night had made her bold, this morning had made her sure. She folded his arm with hers and placed her palm on his solid chest so that his hand covered hers. The steady beat of his heart pulsated beneath her fingertips.

His body was absolutely motionless, but the feel of his supple chest beneath her fingers sent longing shuffling through her. Their only points of contact were his heart beating a throbbing rhythm against her palm and his thigh barely brushing hers.

Her other hand fluttered to his face, and she knew she had stoked a gently growing fire. He lowered his head, finally bringing his lips down to hers. Bekka parted her lips as his mouth claimed hers. She must have been very persuasive, because his mouth moved hungrily over hers.

Her own control, the very purpose for this kiss escaped her. His kiss was utterly familiar, but it contained a new urgency. Their lips parted, and he gazed into her eyes. She brushed a kiss along the corner of his mouth, whispering, "The boys will go to bed in a little while. Stay with me tonight."

He crushed her to him, so tightly she could barely breathe. His heart thundered against hers. His voice dropped in volume but not in intensity. "I can't, Bekka. No one knew I was here last night. No one but you, Jason, and Jimmy. And me. Yet someone threw that brick through the window.''

''You don't know we're the only ones who knew. Mike knew. He called me from the hospital. Maybe someone overheard our conversation, or at least his end of it.''

''You're grasping at straws, Bekka.''

''And you're not?'' Color drained from his face. Too late she realized she'd touched a sore subject.

He straightened, taking a step back. Her hand, the one measuring his heartbeat, fell to her side. ''What are you going to do?'' she asked.

He ran his hand through his hair, his gaze roaming about her house before replying. ''I already know, firsthand, what it's like to pull someone from a burning building. That note said 'Leave or burn.' I won't let you take that chance.''

''What is it with everyone around here?'' she groused. ''Why does everyone try to protect me? I've come to expect it from Mara and Todd. But I won't let you run my life, Conor Bradley.''

''I'm not trying to run your life. I'm trying to save it.''

''So let me save yours back.''

Their spines were both straight, their shoulders squared. They weren't yelling, but their breathing was as ragged as if they were.

''Even if what we shared last night is over, I'd like to help you. You don't have to go.''

''You're wrong, Bekka. I do have to.''

He turned, and she spoke to his back. ''What are you going to do?''

''I'm going to build my house on that lot, just as I planned. I'm going to build my business, nail by nail. And I'm not going to let you and Jimmy and Jason get hurt by being involved with me." With that he spun away from her.

A moment later she heard him murmur good-bye to the kids, heard them call good night before the door closed behind him. "Good," she said to the empty kitchen. He wasn't allowing this person, whoever it was, to run him out of town. But he was walking out of her life, and he claimed to be doing it for her sake. God help her if one more person tried to run her life for her own good.

This isn't over, Conor Bradley. You may be walking out of my life, but as long as you don't walk away from this town, I have time. We both do.

TEN

She should have known Mara wouldn't be caught sleeping in the middle of the day. Bekka's steps had slowed as she passed Rooms 214 and 216. She'd tip-toed over the polished floor at the end of the corridor and opened the door to Room 218 with extra care, in case Mara was asleep. Instead of resting, her sister was seated in a tall-backed hospital chair. Though her face was pale, she was deep in conversation with the nurse.

The young nurse straightened when Bekka entered, and Mara murmured, "Try not to worry. It worked for my cousin, and I'll bet it'll work for you, too."

The nurse's thick-soled shoes didn't make a sound as she took the flowers from Bekka's hands and hurried from the room to find a vase. Bekka watched her go, marveling at her sister's stamina. Little more than a day and a half had lapsed since she'd had emergency surgery, and Mara was already offering her advice to total strangers.

Bekka pulled a chair opposite Mara's and gracefully lowered to its edge. "How are you feeling, Mar?"

Mara took a careful breath and met her gaze. "I've

felt better. And I've felt worse." Her eyes narrowed as she looked at Bekka. "What's wrong, Bek?"

The nurse breezed back into the room with the vase of fresh flowers, saving Bekka from answering. "You two must be sisters," the nurse exclaimed. "You look so much alike."

"We've heard that a time or two, haven't we, Mara?"

"A hundred times," Mara returned. Before the nurse left the room, Mara chided, "Except she's always been skinnier than me. One good thing has resulted from my surgery. I've already lost four pounds."

To herself, Bekka added, *Two good things have resulted from her sister's surgery. Mara was going to be fine, and Conor had spent an entire night with her.* Bekka wondered what Mara would say if she thanked her and realized it didn't matter what Mara said. She wasn't sorry for the time she'd spent in Conor's arms. She wasn't sorry for a single moment of it.

Mara was watching her intently. To escape her sister's shrewd gaze, Bekka rummaged through her purse for her hairbrush. She didn't want to discuss the changes in her appearance, or in her heart, especially not with someone as astute as her only sister. When she found the brush, she handed it to Mara, who immediately raised her hands to her hair and winced as pain knifed through her. Bekka jumped to her feet and began to brush through her sister's short hair.

"I can't even comb my own hair. I'm a weakling," Mara groused.

"Nonsense. You've been sick for a week and underwent surgery less than two days ago. Besides, I think I like having the upper hand for a change. You've tried to be the older sister since the day you were born. I have to take advantage of you when you're down."

Mara's laughter made her wince again. "Oh, Bekky,

don't make me laugh. Besides, I'll never forget you're the older sister. Just wait until you turn thirty.''

''Who's turning thirty?'' Mike asked, pushing the door open to the wall, a half-smile on his lips and a glint in his eyes.

''I am,'' Bekka declared, ''In almost two years. And then, a year later, Mara is. Hi, Mike. How are the kids?''

''Missy and Marc are feeling better, and Mindy's cranky. I think she's coming down with spots. If Mara plays her cards right, she'll miss out on the whole thing.''

''Do you think I planned this?'' Mara wailed.

Mike ignored her in typical husband fashion. ''I just ran into Conor Bradley, Bek, and he said your kitchen is all done.''

''You ran into Conor?'' Bekka asked. ''Where?'' She felt as if a hand had closed around her throat as she waited for Mike to answer.

''Downstairs in the lobby.''

''In this hospital? Is he hurt?'' What if the person who'd written that note had gotten to him? What if Conor had been injured?

Mike shook his head. ''He was asking an orderly questions about any patients who might have come to the emergency room the night Mara had her surgery. Why would you think Conor had been hurt?''

Bekka realized her swift reaction had given her feelings away. Mike and Mara exchanged a look, then turned their intent gazes on her. She wasn't surprised when Mara was the first to speak. ''What's going on, Bek?''

Bekka stared wordlessly at them, the tenderness and worry in their expressions sending tears to her throat. After a long pause, she strode to the open door. She didn't turn back to face them until it had clicked firmly shut.

"Bek, are you all right?" Mara whispered.

"Yes, Mar. I'm fine. I just don't want anyone to overhear."

"Overhear what?"

Bekka spoke to them both, her gaze shifting from one to the other. "You both knew Conor stayed at my house to watch Jimmy and Jason the night before last." Both pairs of eyes were riveted to her face, waiting for her to continue.

"Did you tell anyone?" she asked her brother-in-law.

"Did I tell anyone Conor was at your place?" Mike asked. At her nod, he said, "Your parents are watching the kids now, and your father asked who'd stayed with the boys that night when you came to our house. Was I supposed to keep it a secret?"

"No. I mean, did you tell anyone that night, or early the next morning?"

"Not a soul, Bekka. Why?"

She crossed her arms, then uncrossed them. Settling her hand to the hospital bed, she smoothed a wrinkle from the sheet and answered without looking at either of them. "Someone threw a brick through my window yesterday morning. The note attached was for Conor."

Mara gasped, then clutched her stomach. "What did he say when you showed him?"

Bekka leveled her eyes at her sister and spoke with quiet firmness. "He was there."

Those three words hung in the air for several seconds before Mara sputtered, "All night? He was there all night?"

Bekka let her silence answer her sister's question and looked at Mike, whose attention was suddenly trained on the toe of his worn loafer. He slid his hands into his pockets before meeting her gaze. While Mara was still dumbstruck, he asked, "What did the note say?"

"It said 'Leave. Or burn.' "

A weaker patient might have swooned or fainted. Mara tried to stagger to her feet. She gasped, and Bekka wondered how much of it was from pain and how much was from anxiety and surprise.

"Who sent it?" Mara's and Mike's voices blended with the same question.

"I don't know. I just don't know." Bekka walked to the window. Looking down at the hospital grounds, she said, "No one knew. Except Conor and I and the boys. And the two of you." Her gaze swung to her sister's. "You were in surgery, and unless Mike said something to someone . . ."

"So," Mara grumbled. "Conor really didn't start that fire twelve years ago."

"Of course he didn't."

Mara leaned her head back against the chair and closed her eyes. "You love him. Oh, Bekka, you do. What am I going to do with you?"

Bekka took her time answering. "You're going to respect my judgment and my feelings on this, Mar." *And someday, with a little luck, you're going to respect Conor's, too*, she added to herself.

"This is just like Ted all over again. You wouldn't listen to me that time, either."

Bekka spaced her words evenly. "This is nothing like Ted. *Conor* is nothing like Ted. I loved Ted, but we both know he was selfish. He loved me in his own way, but his needs came before mine. Conor's finished with my kitchen, and I don't expect him back. For my sake, he ended what was between us."

Tears sprang to her eyes, and she did everything she could to blink them away. Mara cocked her head to one side and sniffled, then opened her arms wide to her sister. Bekka went into her embrace, being careful not to hurt her. After a moment Mike cleared his throat. "You know, Bekka," he began, "I did mention the fact that Conor was at your place."

"To who?" Bekka and Mara asked in the same breath.

"Well, not to anyone in particular. It was when I called you, Bek, from the pay phone in the lobby, when I called to tell you Mara's surgery was over and she was going to be all right."

"Who was there?" Bekka asked.

Mike's face contorted as he tried to remember. "No one I knew. Just an old man who was having trouble breathing and a young mother with a sick baby, and maybe a nurse and an orderly or two. No one who looked vicious or demented. No one who looked capable of throwing a brick through a window or of threatening to burn a house down."

A cart squeaked down the hall. A telephone rang and voices rose and fell on the other side of the door. But the hospital room was pin-drop quiet. "What are you going to do?" Mara whispered.

For some reason Bekka's words were spoken on a whisper, too. "I'm going to talk to Conor, tell him we have no idea who could have known he was at my house. Then, I guess all we can do is wait."

Mara groaned. "I've always hated waiting."

Bekka smiled in spite of the graveness of the situation. Mara was notoriously pushy and notoriously impatient when it came to waiting. Shaking her head, Bekka changed the subject. They talked for a few more minutes, and when Mara began to look tired, Bekka said good-bye and left the room.

"Be careful." Mara's words squeezed through the door before it swished closed.

*　　*　　*

Conor's lot was exactly where she expected to find him. Since his back was to her and the deafening drone coming from the yellow backhoe covered the sound of her car's engine, her arrival went undetected. His feet were planted on the grass, a comfortable distance apart. She might have thought he was relaxed, if it wasn't for the hand kneading the muscles at the back of his neck and shoulder.

She parked her car behind his truck and strode to his side in the center of the lot. "He's digging your basement on a Sunday?"

He jumped at the sound of her voice and his gaze swung to hers. She saw his chest expand in surprise, but the tractor covered his startled exclamation.

"He owed me a favor." Conor's words were matter-of-fact. His expression wasn't. An unexpected warmth surged through her at the look in his eyes, and she almost smiled. Then his eyes darkened, and she realized he was pulling away from her.

Bekka swallowed hard, trying to muster her courage. She'd chosen her clothes carefully. Red and white. Brave colors. She knew the rose blush accented her cheekbones, knew the brown mascara shaded her eyes. And she knew the exact moment his gaze settled on her lips she'd painstakingly tinted a dark ruby. For a moment she read invitation in the smoldering depths of his eyes. But the moment passed.

"You shouldn't be here, Bekka. I thought I made myself clear."

"I'm here on business."

His look said, "I'll just bet." Stubborn man.

Bekka raised her chin and met his gaze. "I'm thinking about remodeling the upstairs of my house, and I'd like you to give me an estimate." She hadn't really planned to begin the project until the following summer. But darn him, she needed a reason to see him, a reason to stay close, to show him, over and over, he wasn't alone.

"Yeah, well . . ." he gestured to the lot. "I'm going to be pretty tied up with this project and the others I'm already contracted to finish. But I'd be happy to send one of our builders over to take a look."

"I only want you."

She drew in a deep breath and forbade herself to tremble at his response to her words. His eyelids closed and his lips parted as he sucked in a deep breath. She studied his face feature by feature and doubted she'd ever forget a single detail. Not his square chin or dark hair, not the undignified shadow on his cheeks, certainly not the intense look in his blue eyes, and not his wide mouth, which, when pressed to hers, had a power all its own.

"Oh, Bekka. What am I going to do with you?" he rasped.

She leaned closer. "I have a few suggestions."

Her heart thudded noisily within her as she waited for his response. She saw the battles taking place behind his eyes. In the end, his common sense won. Disappointed, Bekka swung away from him. After taking a few steps, she turned her body halfway and called over the machine's rumble, "Just an informal estimate, Conor. Just you and me. We'll begin with my bedroom." Before turning around, she added, "Tonight, Conor, I'll see you then."

She made her way to her car, the narrow heels of her red pumps poking into the grassy lot. She knew his gaze followed her, could feel it with every step she took. It warmed her back, warmed her shoulders beneath the thin fabric of her red blouse, warmed the dip of her spine and the skin beneath her white slacks.

Upon reaching her car, she grasped the steering wheel with both hands to keep them from shaking.

Without a backward glance, she pulled away from the curb.

Watching her go, Conor had no intention of showing up on her doorstep later that night on the pretense of measuring for closet space. *Just you and me. We'll begin with my bedroom.* Heat surged beneath his skin, and he was glad no one was around to witness his body's reaction. *I only want you.* When she'd said that, he'd almost lost the last shred of self-restraint he possessed. She wanted him, dammit. It stoked his ego, his desire, and his unease over the message on that stinking brick.

He jerked his head around to the backhoe and tried to concentrate on its progress. He paced to the edge of the hole where his basement would be and back again, trying not to think about the tightness in his body. Hell, he wasn't even sure where the ache started. In his heart. Or much, much lower.

"A little farther," Bekka directed.

"How's this?"

"A little more."

"Like this?" Conor asked.

"Ah, perfect," she crooned.

The sound went straight to his senses, which in turn dove straight to one particular area of his body, which had been pulsating like a warrior's drum ever since she'd walked away this afternoon. He knocked on the wall they were measuring and said, "There are a couple of different ways we could do this."

"Such as?"

Hell and damnation. Conor ran his hand through his hair and gave up trying to pretend he didn't know what she was doing. He shook his head in her direction, then dragged his gaze from hers to the wall in question. He should have told her to cut it out, but he didn't want her to stop. He should have told her in no uncertain terms he wouldn't come over tonight. But he couldn't stay away.

Only one thing, with one woman, would ease the knot in him. Not running a hundred miles, not all the physical labor in the world. Only Bekka could give him what he needed.

He clenched his jaw, releasing the lock on the tape measure. It automatically rewound, snapping when it reached the end. He placed the measure inside the proper pocket of his tool belt lying on an old trunk and sank down beside it.

She wanted him. She made it painfully, achingly clear. Bekka was the only woman he wanted, and he wanted to keep her from harm. Those two wants were poles apart. One couldn't be obtained without jeopardizing the other.

Bekka's heart thudded at the weariness in Conor's eyes, in his shoulders. She watched his expression sorrowfully, brushing her hair from her forehead where it clung to her warm skin. The temperature and humidity were on the rise again. Even though night had fallen, the rooms upstairs still felt the heaviness of the day's heat, just as her heart felt the heaviness of an indelible, unattainable love.

She sat next to him on the trunk and slid her feet from her sandals. Although he made no move to touch her, she was aware of the hardness of his thigh so near her own. She was also aware that unless she could reach him, he'd leave.

She crossed her legs, slowly following the contour of his shin with the arch of her foot. Her bare foot reached an area just below his knee, then dipped down again. Her gaze climbed from her toes to the naked longing in his eyes. She laid her palm on his knee and heard his sharp intake of breath. His hand covered hers, and she felt every layer, the layer of denim covering his skin, the layer of skin on her own palm covering his jean-clad thigh, and his work-roughened hand covering hers. He was like those layers, each a different texture, every one unique, rich, and warm.

She looked up into his face, saw the longing in his gaze and the tension that longing created. Opening her eyes wide, she drank in the care and tenderness, wishing there was some way to banish thoughts of that fire all those years ago, wishing there was some way to make him forget about that brick and broken glass, at least for one night.

A sound, low and primal, came from someplace deep inside him. He touched a finger to her cheek and wiped a tear away, a tear she wasn't aware had fallen. His lips brushed her cheek and skimmed along her jaw before settling to her mouth.

He kissed her, and feelings shivered along her spine. He whispered her name against her mouth. She answered by offering him everything a woman could give a man.

"What am I going to do about you?" His voice rasped in her ear, sending a tiny smile to her lips.

She relaxed against him, sliding her arms around his back. Relief made her giddy. He wasn't immune to her. Far from it. "Oh, Conor," she murmured, "Mara asked me that same question earlier today."

He stiffened, and Bekka wanted to call back her words. They reminded him of her family, of the harm he was trying to keep from her. He set her away from him and, picking up his tool belt, strode around to the other side of her bed.

He stopped in the doorway and stood there, straight and tall. "You told Mara about that note?"

Taking a steadying breath, she pushed to her feet. She didn't answer until she stood only a few feet from him. "Yes. I also asked Mike if anyone might have overheard him say you were here the night Mara had her surgery."

"Did anyone overhear him?"

"He said there were a couple of people waiting for treatment in the emergency room, and a few of the hospital staff. But there was nobody there who looked suspicious, nobody who looked vicious. I don't get it, Conor. Who else knew?"

The hammer dangled from the tool belt, clanking against the floor as Conor's other hand went to the muscles in the back of his neck. "I don't know. But someone had to know."

He glanced around the room before continuing. "If you're serious about remodeling the upstairs, I'll have one of the other carpenters take a look at it. Until I know who threw that brick and why, I won't jeopardize your safety."

She didn't know how to argue with that kind of logic. "What about your own safety?"

"I'm tough as nails, Bekka."

She wanted to tell him she knew better, knew he was tough on the outside but warm and tender where it counted, in his heart. Bekka opened her mouth to speak, but he spoke first.

"I told Mac about the second note. He thinks I should ask Vince a few questions."

"Vince? Why him?"

"Because Mac thinks those notes have something to do with the rumors that started twelve years ago. And because he says things are rarely what they seem."

Bekka had to fight her own battle of restraint to keep from hurling herself into his arms. She worried for his safety and ached because he was facing danger alone. She squeezed his hand, hoping to convey in that one touch everything she couldn't say.

He turned at her words and almost smiled. "I was born careful, remember?" A moment later he disappeared down the back stairway, strode across her new kitchen, and went out the back door.

The porch light came on as soon as Conor knocked. Vince stood inside the screen door. Conor stood outside. Neither said anything for a long moment, each measuring the other. "Can I come in?" Conor finally asked.

"Suit yourself."

Jagged thoughts plagued Conor as he opened the door and stepped into the kitchen. Looking around, he took in the old furnishings, the ancient white refrigerator and the old Formica-topped table. It was clean and neat and far from warm, even with the hot July weather.

"You might as well ask."

Conor delved Vince's expression for the meaning behind his words. Vince shook his head twice and went to lean against the counter.

"Ask, dammit." Vince's voice shook with a raw, primitive anger, one that had evidently never died.

Conor stared straight into his eyes across the kitchen, straight into the eyes of the kid who'd been his best friend, his only friend, straight into the eyes of the kid who'd knocked him cold in a fit of blind fury. Conor knew. In his gut he knew he wasn't staring at a man who'd thrown a brick through Bekka's front window.

Vince hadn't moved since he'd spoken, not even to blink. Conor's hoarse voice broke the silence between them. "I don't have to ask. I know it wasn't you."

Vince's eyes narrowed. "Then why are you here?"

Conor ran his hand through his hair, down the back of his neck, then handed the note to Vince. "There's a question. I'm not sure, but this all has something to do with me. And something to do with you."

Conor pulled a chair out and sat, his knees apart, forearms resting on his thighs. "You were in uniform the last time you saw this note. You're not in uniform now. Any idea what this is about?"

Vince stared at the message on that sheet of paper for a long time. "Someone doesn't want you here."

He handed the note back to Conor, and Conor stared at the other man, searching for something in his manner, in his eyes, searching for a clue to something he might know. If Vince knew something, it didn't show, not in his face, not in his manner.

After a moment of wrestling with his thoughts Conor leaned back and said, "The place looks the same."

"Yeah, well, you know what they say, home is where the heart is." Vince's tone was sarcastic. He pulled out a chair and hiked one shoe on its seat.

"Your mother tried."

"When it came to my old man, her best just wasn't good enough, was it?"

"This place was a helluva lot homier than mine," Conor stated, remembering the filth and clutter of his childhood home.

Vince leaned both arms on his bent knee. His left brow rose a fraction as he said, "Let's face it, Conor. Both our childhoods were rotten! And it wasn't because of the houses we lived in. If it wasn't for your old man, we both would have lived in that old apple tree in your backyard, and you know it." Vince's voice had faded, losing its steely edge.

Conor stretched his legs out, bringing one ankle up to rest on his knee. He hadn't thought about that in a long, long time. When they were about eight years old, they'd wanted to build a tree house in Conor's apple tree, wanted to live there together. They'd even found some scrap lumber and rusty nails and had started on the floor.

Vince must have been thinking about it, too, because he said, ''You were a builder even then.''

They'd hurried home from school to find the boards splintered, a broken heap on the ground, and Conor's father furious. He'd hauled Vince home by the scruff of his neck, the yelling match between Sam Bradley and Leroy Macelli the talk of the neighborhood for days. Those two men had hated each other even then; the fact that they couldn't force that hatred onto their sons was a constant thorn in their sides. In the end, their fathers had won. In the end, the boys had lost, and Vince's fist had severed their friendship.

In the end, Gloria Macelli had a black eye, and Conor had feared she'd had a broken spirit. Conor's house had burned, and he and his father had cleared out. His father may have given Conor life, but Conor had saved Sam Bradley's life the night of the fire. As far as they were both concerned, that made them even. Conor found them a cheap room in Detroit, and Sam never raised a hand to him again. When Sam died the following year, Conor found a job with Mac and moved to a better place. He hadn't seen any of the Macellis for twelve years, but he'd thought of them often.

''I always felt sorry for your mother,'' Conor murmured.

''Yeah, I know.''

''Where'd she go?'' Conor asked.

''Moved to Lansing the same summer you left. I went with her. She divorced my old man, got a job in an insurance office, and ended up marrying her boss.''

''No kidding?''

''Yeah,'' Vince said sheepishly. ''He treats her like a queen, too.''

So Gloria Macelli had finally found happiness. Conor was glad.

''Heard your old man had a heart attack the year after

you left." Conor nodded and Vince added, "Funny. I never knew he had a heart."

"What about your father?" Conor asked.

"My mother got the house. After I finished my police training, she gave it to me, so good old Leroy moved into a run-down trailer behind the junkyard south of town. Being a policeman, I run into him now and then, but he has nothing to do with me, doesn't even acknowledge that I'm his son. His smoking finally got to him. He fights for every breath he takes, holding onto life with every ornery bone in his body. As if he ever had a life."

Vince let his foot drop to the floor, and Conor stood. Memories of Vince's father ended the conversation, ended the visit. It was the most they'd spoken in over twelve years, but their conversation hadn't healed the rift in their friendship. Both of them knew it would take a miracle to do that.

Conor slid the note into his pocket and ambled toward the door. "Neither one of us intended to come back to this neighborhood. Yet here we both are. You're living in your father's house . . ."

"And you're building a house on your father's lot." Vince finished Conor's statement.

"How did you know I'm building a house on that lot?"

"Millerton isn't a large city, Conor. I heard it through the grapevine. Also heard Bekka's boys were climbing that apple tree. You planning on building your house big enough for them?"

"No." It was true. Conor couldn't imagine Bekka living in the house he was building. He couldn't even imagine himself living there. When he'd first walked into this kitchen, Vince had said home is where the heart is. Looking around, Conor saw very little of Vince's heart here.

Vince must have been thinking along the same line. "I think our ancestors had the right idea."

"Our ancestors?" Conor asked.

"Apes. They lived in trees. Maybe we should, too."

Or in tree houses. Conor didn't know where the thought came from. On its heels came another. Vince hadn't acted surprised Conor had shown up tonight. In fact, it was as if he'd been expecting him.

They stared at each other for a long moment before Conor finally turned to leave. He let the door bang shut behind him, its echo taking the place of good-bye.

Something about this whole situation didn't add up. It never had. He climbed into his Chevy and headed toward his rented house across town.

Vince had as good as said his house wasn't his home. Conor knew the feeling. He'd lived in the suburbs of Detroit for twelve years, but had never thought of it as home. His apartment didn't feel like home either. He was building a house on a lot that was legally his, but he knew legality had nothing to do with feeling at home.

Home wasn't a place, but a feeling. He'd taken one look at Bekka and had felt the pull of her smile. Day after day she'd drawn him, like lamplight to a weary traveler. Wherever Bekka was, that was home.

Conor pushed in the clutch and felt the note in his pocket crinkle. That note reminded him he couldn't go to Bekka. He couldn't go home. Not until he knew what he was dealing with. Not until he knew who.

ELEVEN

"Conor! Look at me!" Jason called from the back of the lot.

Stopping his hammer in mid-swing, Conor turned his head toward the boys, who were racing around the old vines and bushes near the apple tree. Their laughter twittered through the dusk, their voices tapping Conor's heart like a woodpecker pecking bark.

More than a week had passed since he'd measured the walls in Bekka's upstairs. Quite possibly the longest week of his life. He'd known how much he'd missed her, but until this moment, he hadn't realized how much he'd missed her boys. She'd stopped by on her own earlier in the week, just to say hi, she said. That time, like tonight, she'd filled paper cups with lemonade from a thermos, offering him something cold to drink. That time, like tonight, her eyes were filled with a curious longing, and he knew lemonade wasn't all she was offering.

Lemonade was all he'd accepted then. It was all he'd accept tonight.

Bekka leaned against the two-by-fours while Conor

nailed support beams into place. Even though he only worked on it evenings and weekends, the construction of his house was progressing at a surprising rate. The basement blocks were laid, and the first-floor joists and partitions were in. He'd said he'd build a house, sturdy and strong. Leaning against a thick beam, she knew he was doing just that. He'd also said he had to stay away from her. True to his word, he'd walked out of her house last Sunday, and he hadn't been back.

She understood. He wanted to keep her safe, far away from harm. She knew he couldn't offer her shared tomorrows, not until he dealt with his alone. She knew it, and that knowledge made her afraid.

"I heard you went to see Vince."

"How'd you hear that?"

"Through the grapevine," she replied. Conor certainly hadn't told her. She'd gotten it from Mara, who'd gotten it from Dustin, who'd seen Conor's truck parked in front of Vince's place.

She waited for Conor to comment and knew it could be a long wait. Dusk was fast turning into darkness, and she should have been getting Jimmy and Jason home and into bed. But she couldn't leave, not until she knew whether he'd received any more threats.

"What did Vince say about that note?"

"Not much."

"I see. And have you received any more . . ." Her voice trailed away into thin air.

Conor took his time forming an answer. He drove another nail, then slid his hammer through the loop on the carpenter's apron. She didn't think he was going to reply. When he did, the words were spoken so softly, she barely heard.

He'd said yes.

"And?"

He finally met her gaze, and Bekka realized it was

the look in his eyes that had brought her senses back to life the first time he'd stepped foot in her house. It was the look in his eyes that made her heart ache right now. "Another note?" At his nod, she asked, "The same message?"

He unhooked his tool belt before replying. "Identical. Except this time it came through *my* window, and this time it was attached to a twisted old pipe instead of a brick."

She wanted to go to him, to put her arms around him. She wanted to offer him comfort, to be comforted in return. One look at his face told her it was no use. He wasn't letting her close. "It came through your window? When?"

He kneaded the muscle in the back of his neck and whispered, "Last night." His voice grew stronger with his next words. "Bekka, you have to stay away from here. I still don't know for sure who's doing this. But this person is dangerous. Promise me you and the boys will stay away. Until this is over. Promise."

No! sprang to her lips, but she couldn't bring herself to say it out loud. Weariness deepened his eyes, lines of fatigue etched his face, and the strain of the past several months stiffened his shoulders. He had enough to worry about without having to worry about her. "All right, Conor. I promise."

The kids came running from the backyard, informing him his apple tree was the best tree in the world, before scrambling into the backseat of the car. From their open windows, they called good-bye. He answered with a grin before his gaze turned to Bekka's. Neither of them said good-bye, but she offered him a smile warm enough to glide through butter. He loaded his tools into his truck and climbed inside. Through her rear view mirror she watched him pull away from the curb behind her, saw him turn in the opposite direction.

By promising to stay away, even these little visits were off limits, and Bekka wondered when she'd see him again. "Stay away until this is over," he'd said. She wondered what it would take to *be over*.

The notes had said "Leave. Or burn." Conor wasn't leaving. An image flashed through her mind, and fear, so real she could taste it, gripped her body. If Conor didn't leave, would he burn?

It was past midnight, but the image of Conor, engulfed in flames, tormented her. Jimmy and Jason had been sound asleep for hours, but Bekka knew there was no sense even trying to sleep. She brewed herself a pot of tea, something she rarely did in the summertime, and carried it to the front porch.

A three-quarter moon lit the yard. The swing creaked, and the wind murmured across the fields. She took a sip of her tea, then went still. Straining her ears, she listened for several seconds. Not a sound could be heard, except blood pounding in her ears. She placed her palm to her heart, which suddenly felt two sizes too large for her body. For a moment she thought she'd heard a siren. A fire siren.

Distant headlights came steadily closer. Gravel crunched beneath tires as a car turned into her driveway. Bekka ran to the porch railing, then sailed down the steps as Mara stepped from her car. "Mara, what's wrong?" Dread dropped like a weight to her stomach as she waited for her sister's reply.

"A fire."

"Where?"

"At Conor's house."

A thread of hysteria wove its way through Bekka's mind, along with the image of flames. She breathed in shallow gasps of air. "Did he get out? Mara, tell me he's safe."

"Not his apartment house, Bek. Someone set fire to the house he's building."

"His house! But why? He wouldn't be there at night."

"He's probably there now, Bek, and if he was the man I loved, I'd want to be there with him."

Tears brimmed in Bekka's eyes, and a sob escaped the lump in her throat. "Oh, Mar."

"You can 'Oh, Mar' me later, right after Mike's through with me."

Mara claimed she'd recovered from her surgery, but Bekka knew it took more than ten days to heal. Evidently Mike hadn't wanted her to come tonight. Bekka didn't know whether to throttle her sister for coming or kiss her. In her haste, she did neither. "You'll stay with Jimmy and Jason?"

"Why else do you think I came?"

Bekka hurried inside. Mara followed more slowly. Taking her purse from the shelf, Bekka issued direct orders that Mara take it easy, not stopping to think until she was out of the house, in her car, and heading toward town two miles away, toward the sirens in the distance, toward Conor.

The entire neighborhood was lit up. Yellow light spilled from every window. Red lights of a fire engine flashed up ahead, along with the red and blue lights of a police car. Bekka took the first available parking spot nearly two blocks from the fire and started to run.

Neighbors stood in their robes on front stoops. Others were huddled on the sidewalk, nearly blocking her path. A night wind blew the smoke her way, the fumes clinging to her hair, stinging her nose and throat. Bekka dodged the spectators, her eyes trained on the flames lighting the sky, her eyes searching for Conor.

There was no mistaking the man standing near the side of the lot. Others were huddled in groups. Conor stood alone. His hands were buried in his pockets. His shoulders were squared, his spine as straight as the boards he'd nailed into place, the boards that were now engulfed in flames. A sob rose in Bekka's throat as she hurried toward him.

Her breathing was sharp and uneven. Her eyes were brimming with tears, from the smoke, from the desolation of the fire, and from the anguish of Conor's pain.

"Who?" she cried. "Who did this?"

He pulled his gaze from the flames, but Bekka saw them reflected in his eyes. For a moment he simply shook his head. When he found his voice, it was so deep, it shook. "Bud Trierweller called me. Right after he called the fire station. He doesn't know how it started. But I do. I just don't know who."

Neither of them said another word, but Bekka didn't leave his side. They watched as the volunteer fire fighters pointed their hoses at the flames, as the smoke bucked against the water, hissing and writhing like a huge black snake. Bekka had never realized how loud a fire was. Flames cracked the night, water gushed from hoses, spilling onto boards and cement like a waterfall crashing over rocks.

She gradually became aware of another presence. Vince Macelli stared at the fire for several seconds without saying anything. He was in uniform, evidently on duty tonight. Bekka watched his profile, wondering whose face wore the greater look of anguish. His or Conor's.

As if someone flicked a switch, the night was suddenly quiet. The fire was out, the hoses turned off. For a moment, everyone, the fire fighters, the spectators, Vince and Conor and Bekka, stared where the flames had been. Then everyone began talking at once. The fire chief spoke to Bud Trierweller, to other neighbors, to Conor, and to Vince. The firemen rolled up their hoses and the truck finally pulled away. Neighbors talked among themselves before slowly making their way into their houses.

The silence between the three remaining people was nearly as thick as the smoke had been. Bekka had no way of knowing what Conor and Vince were thinking. They stared at each other across the silence of twelve years. Were they thinking about the fire tonight? Or the fire that had burned the house to the ground twelve years ago?

"I'll leave you two alone," Bekka murmured.

Before she'd taken more than two steps, Vince's words stopped her. "No, Bekka. You don't have to go." Then, to Conor, he said, "I have to talk to you. But not tonight. First, there's someone I need to see."

"What is it, Macelli?" Conor asked in a harsh, raw voice.

"I'm on duty tonight. I'll tell you as soon as I can." With that, Vince strode to the police car and drove away, and Bekka and Conor were alone.

The moon was their only source of light, the streetlight on the corner unable to penetrate the darkness here. Bekka stood close to Conor, questions strumming through her mind, all of them leading to one thought. "Do you think Vince is responsible after all?"

"I don't know. But Vince knows, or at least suspects someone."

He cast a look at the place where the walls of his house had been. Bekka did the same. "You promised you'd stay away from here."

Her throat felt raw with unuttered protests. Until that moment, she'd forgotten about her promise. Making sure Conor was safe had overridden all else. "Are you sorry I came?" She heard the weariness in her own voice, the fear, the confusion, and the love. "Are you, Conor?"

She couldn't see him clearly in the darkness, at least not with her eyes. Instead, she saw with her heart the battle taking place inside him. Bekka felt as if she were holding her breath, waiting for his answer, waiting for him to admit his feelings for her were real.

The shake of his head was barely discernible, but it was enough. Hope surged within her. He wasn't sorry she was there.

"Neither am I." She raised her chin and squared her shoulders. If he told her she should be sorry, she'd throttle him. She needn't have worried. He didn't say another word. But then, words weren't necessary. There was a tangible bond between them, one that had grown stronger with every passing day.

His hand trailed from her elbow to her wrist before entwining her fingers with his own. His nearness kindled feelings only he could ignite. With a gentle hand, he pulled her with him, toward the shadows at the back of the lot, toward the overgrown bushes and tangled vines. He didn't stop until he'd reached the apple tree.

Not a single moonbeam filtered through the thick leaves overhead. Not a porch light was lit, not a window illuminated. Only darkness surrounded them. Darkness, and feelings neither could deny. His hand found her hair, hers slid up his chest. She breathed in the scent of smoke and relished the beating of his heart beneath her palm. He paused to kiss her, whispering, "I love you."

Her heart swelled to bursting, pleasure radiating outward. He loved her. She'd suspected, hoped for, and yearned for his love. He was giving it to her now. She breathed between parted lips, answering on a sigh, "And I love you."

He kissed her so deeply every muscle in her body went soft. She kissed him in return, drawing his love from him and giving hers back again. Bekka felt him tug his shirt from his jeans, heard at least one button pop as he yanked the rest free in one motion. Then his chest was bare and he gathered her close, wrapping his arms around her. His heart quaked in her ear, and she turned her head, pressing her lips to his skin, feeling his heartbeat beneath her kiss.

She wore a cotton dress, drop-waisted and knee-skimming. While he spread his shirt on the grass, she slipped out of her dress and laid it next to his shirt. Together they dropped to their knees, then farther down until they rested face to face on their sides, their clothing like a sheet underneath them.

The breeze stirred the leaves overhead, rustled the bushes and grapevines all around them, but didn't penetrate their seclusion. Bekka slipped her sandals from her feet, and Conor's hand slid over her waist, slowly climbing higher. She heard him take a deep breath when he discovered she wasn't wearing a bra, and she felt his smile against her own lips.

He kissed the hollow at the base of her neck, then dipped lower to her breast. His shirt was smooth beneath her hair and shoulders, her dress a slightly different texture beneath the rest of her. Her eyelids fluttered down when Conor moved to her other breast, the July air warm where it touched her sensitized flesh. She inhaled the scent of smoke lingering in his hair and pressed a kiss to the top of his head. With a moan of pleasure, he raised his head and found her lips once more.

His kisses made her bold, his touch made her eager. She glided her hands over him, over his shoulders, then back again, down his back, across the flatness of his stomach. Her fingers dipped beneath the low-riding waistband of his jeans, and the muscles deep in his belly contracted. He cupped her shoulders with both hands, pressing her back to the ground, and whisked her panties from her hips before deftly unfastening his belt and gliding his zipper down.

Bekka wished she could see him, wished she could make out his expression, his male body, so bold and proud. He lay down beside her, naked, partially covering her with his chest, and her hands explored what her eyes couldn't see.

He whispered into her hair, indiscernible words that made her senses soar. She rolled to her side as Conor rolled to his back, bringing her on top of him. For a moment she lay perfectly still, marveling at the body beneath hers. She kissed his neck, breathed in his scent, a scent that could never be bottled, the scent of soap and sawdust and man, a scent touched with smoke tonight. She began to move, kissing and touching and feeling.

His hands found her waist, and he lifted her onto him, her hair falling over her shoulders like a curtain. She closed her eyes as fiery sensations ricocheted through her, feeling herself stretch to accept all of him. Pressing her hands to his shoulders, she began to move, the sounds coming from someplace deep in his throat spurring her on. His hands moved over her breasts, and she strained against them. With the first tiny explosions, she increased the tempo.

His hands slid to her waist, where he held her fast and matched her every move with one of his own. They both cried out on a whisper, their love and their passion transporting them to a place all their own. They stayed there, together, heartbeat to heartbeat, until the night sounds called them back to earth.

Bekka didn't know exactly how she'd gotten to her side, tucked against the curve of Conor's body. Her breathing gradually returned to normal, and her eyelids opened partway. Fireflies sparked above them, and the wind murmured through the leaves overhead like a love song.

Conor smoothed her hair off her forehead and cheeks. "This tree was my favorite place when I was a kid. I think it's my favorite place now."

"You think?" she teased.

His voice lost that teasing quality. His next words were spoken on a whisper, deep and mournful. "My house is gone."

"You can rebuild."

"Can I? Can a person ever really start over?"

"I did. You can, too."

"You're beautiful. Warm and kind. You were kind to me that other time, too."

Bekka wrapped her arms around his waist, hugging him with all her might. "This was no act of kindness, Conor. What we just shared was an act of love."

There was something undeniably special between them, a bond that went beyond desire, a bond that had been tremulously formed twelve years ago when she'd helped him stagger into the house on this very lot. He thought he'd lost everything he had that night when fire had destroyed his house. What his father hadn't managed to wring out of him throughout his childhood Vince had crushed with his fist the night of the fire.

Conor had thought there was nothing left for him here. His house was gone, his friendship with Vince shattered. But before he left, a girl with sky-blue eyes had given him something precious. He'd been delirious and had barely remembered, but he'd never forgotten either. Bekka had smiled at him that night, and in her smile, a bond had formed, a bond that transcended the physical.

She'd been a girl then. She was a woman now. He kissed her and felt her smile on his own lips. "You looked into my eyes that night, Bekka, and you smiled, just as you're smiling now." His voice was low and deep, almost as low and deep as the memories he'd buried twelve years ago.

"Tell me about that night, Conor. Tell me what happened."

The hand that had been stroking her hair stilled. She wished she could look into his face in the darkness, wished she could read his expression. All she could do was listen, and remain perfectly motionless, and wait.

"It was dark outside. And stifling hot. My father came home in a raging temper. I steered clear until he passed out, then escaped to the front stoop. Nothing was going on in the neighborhood, so I decided to walk on over to Vince's.

"Lights were on in the house, and raised voices rang through the open windows. I stood outside the screen door, and what I saw sickened me." Conor grew silent, lost in painful memories. When he continued, that pain was there in his voice, like a rasp, a sore that still hadn't healed. "Vince's mother was crying. Her dress was ripped off her shoulder and her face was swollen and bruised. Vince's father was clutching his hand as if it was broken and kicking anything in his path.

"Vince was crying. I'd never seen him cry. Not even when we were kids. He saw me through the screen door, and something inside him seemed to snap. He rushed toward me, and I lunged backwards, stumbling off the steps.

" 'What did he do to her?' I screamed. 'What did your father do to her?'

"I took a backward step for every step Vince took toward me. I'd never seen such a look of hatred, such unbridled anger. Rage scathed his voice as he told me her face was swollen because *my* old man hit her. Right after he tried to force himself on her."

Bekka felt physically sick. That poor woman. And

those poor boys. No one should have to endure what Gloria Macelli had endured that night. No boys should have to witness it.

"And Vince came after you?" she asked.

"What could I say to him? 'Sorry, man, I'm sure my old man didn't mean anything by it.' Nothing I could have said would have made any difference. Nothing I could do would undo what my father had already done. So, I turned and ran. Vince caught up with me in my front yard. I was no match for his fury. The fist I took in my stomach staggered me. The one to my jaw knocked me cold."

Bekka pressed her fingers to her mouth to keep from crying out. Tears welled in her eyes, tears for the boys Conor and Vince had been, and tears for the men they were today. They were scarred by their childhoods, bruised by what they'd seen.

"That's when I found you, isn't it, Conor? After Vince had hit you. You were innocent, you know. He lashed out at you for the sins of your father. And I doubt he's forgiven himself, even after all these years."

Dew was forming on their bare skin, and Bekka shivered. They both sat up and groped through the dark for their clothes. She stood, shrugged into her loose-fitting dress, then bent to slip her feet into her sandals. His zipper rasped and his belt buckle creaked. Then his hand slid around her waist.

She rested her head on his shoulder and he whispered, "Later that same night, after you helped me inside, the house caught fire, and everything went up in smoke."

They walked to the soggy rubble in the middle of his lot. "This is the second time a house has burned on this lot. This time it was deliberately set."

"Vince?" she asked.

"I don't think so."

"Then who?"

"I have an idea. But only the person responsible knows for sure."

He walked her to her car and kissed her with such tenderness she feared she'd melt into a heap before him. "Come home with me, Conor."

"I can't." He leaned his forehead against hers and whispered, "I love you, Bekka. I've never said those words before tonight. Not to anyone. But until I talk to Vince tomorrow, until I know who's doing this, I can't risk your safety."

She kissed him tenderly, her fingers gliding down his face like a whisper. He made sure she buckled her seat belt, then closed her door with a firm click. "Only for a little while longer, Bekka. It's almost over. All this . . ." he motioned to his lot, ". . . is almost over."

"Until tomorrow," she called through her open window.

"Until tomorrow," he returned. "Until tomorrow."

Bekka parked inside the garage, the moon lighting her way over the sidewalk. She noticed the pile of scrap lumber lying near the garage and made a mental note to borrow her father's pickup truck this week and haul the wood away.

She tiptoed into her home and was relieved to find Mara asleep on the sofa. With a gentle shake to her shoulder, Mara awoke. "What is it? What? Oh, Bekky, it's you," she mumbled.

"You can stay all night if you'd like, Mar."

Muffling a huge yawn, Mara murmured, "No, thanks. I can't sleep soundly unless Mike is close by. What time is it anyway?"

"After two."

"It took this long to put out that fire?"

"No," Bekka answered. "It's been out for a long

time." It hadn't taken long to put out the house fire, but Bekka knew it would take forever to put out the fire Conor had started deep inside her. Even after a lifetime, she doubted the flame of desire between them would dwindle.

"Ah ha," Mara answered shrewdly. "Is he all right?"

"Yes, he's fine."

"I'll just bet."

Bekka shook her head and murmured, "Thanks for coming, Mara."

"What are sisters for?" Mara replied. "How did it start, anyway?"

"It was set."

Mara gasped. "Oh, Bekka, who?"

"By a person whose hatred has twisted his mind and burned his soul."

"Do you know who that person is?"

"I have a pretty good idea. I think Conor does, too."

"Who?" Mara screeched.

"I can't tell you, Mar. Not yet. First, Conor has to talk to Vince."

"Vince Macelli? But Vince and Conor were best friends. What does Vince have to do with this?"

"I'll tell you as soon as I know for sure."

Mara sputtered about being kept in the dark, about coming over in spite of her husband's protests that she was too weak, about coming to her sister's rescue only to be forced to wait to find out what was going on. Bekka smiled at her sister's impatience. "I'll tell you, Mar, as soon as I know. I promise."

Bekka saw Mara out to her car, waving as she drove away. She checked on Jimmy and Jason, then stepped beneath the shower, washing the smell of smoke from her hair and skin before crawling into bed. Her last thought before drifting off to sleep was *Soon this will all be over, and Conor and I can be together. Forever.*

Over breakfast the following morning Bekka told Jimmy and Jason about the fire at Conor's lot. They were amazed to learn Aunt Mara had come and gone without their knowledge and some bad person had set Conor's house on fire. Jason indignantly chastised the unknown "bad guy," but Jimmy stared into her eyes without saying a word. She reassured them both that Conor would be fine, that he'd find out who had done it, but silently worried about what she saw in her older son's expression. He looked worried and confused and, for reasons she didn't understand, hurt.

She sent the boys out to play but couldn't shake the feeling of unease surrounding her. As she was taking sheets from the clothesline later that morning, Jason's undiluted hero worship rang loud and clear as he talked about Conor.

"Conor could take on ten bad guys!" he crowed. "He could beat 'em all."

Preoccupied, Jimmy didn't reply.

"When's lunch, Mommy?" Jason called. "Me and Jimmy are starving."

"Jimmy and I," she corrected automatically. "Ten minutes," she added with a smile, thinking even the bravest heroes had to eat. Her younger son hopped from his bike, then skipped ahead into the house. She ruffled his straight hair when he passed and reminded Jimmy to come inside, too.

Half an hour later she stacked their plates and carried them into the kitchen. Her rubber-soled shoes squeaked on the new linoleum when she walked to the wastebasket and automatically brushed the crumbs from the plates, forgetting to use her new disposal. It seemed everything she did this morning she did automatically. Her thoughts were never far from Conor. How long before he talked to Vince, how long before the fires were completely doused? She placed the dishes on the counter and took a deep breath.

Smoke stung her nostrils.

Black clouds of smoke poured into the house through the screen. Bekka dashed through the side door and down the steps, nearly running over Jimmy and Jason in her haste.

She plunged into action at the sight of the woodpile engulfed in flames. "Boys. Run to the oak tree. And stay there," she commanded. Fear rounded their eyes, but they did as they were told.

Smoke curled and billowed into the sky. Fueled by the breeze, orange flames licked the bricks on the garage wall and consumed the old lumber on the pile nearby. Bekka pointed the garden hose at the flames, dousing the garage wall and roof, the old lumber and rubble. Flames hissed at the deluge of water. Angry smoke writhed, fighting against the streaming water.

In a matter of minutes, it was out. The fire was silenced, extinguished. Bekka continued to spray the entire area, fearing fire's potential for destruction.

She looked down the driveway at her sons, who were huddled together beneath the oak tree. *Leave. Or burn.* She hadn't believed that person had meant her. Thank goodness the kids had been in the house with her. Thank goodness she'd gotten to the fire before it spread. Relief coursed through her. On its heels, a new fear snaked down her spine.

TWELVE

Bekka eased Jimmy's head to the pillow and slid her arms from his narrow shoulders. She covered his sleeping form with a summer blanket and placed her fingers to her lips. "Sh," she whispered to Jason before taking his hand and leading him from the family room.

Jimmy's reaction to the fire had her worried. He'd wept uncontrollably, finally falling into a fitful sleep in the middle of the afternoon. She'd done everything she could to reassure both boys they were safe. Jason was usually quicker to tears, but today Jimmy had been almost impossible to console.

Bekka didn't know what to do. Calling the fire department now seemed useless. Should she report the fire to the police? What could they do about it now that it was over?

She wanted to talk to Conor, but when she called Pearson Construction, the secretary said he wasn't in. Jason wanted her attention, so she took a deck of playing cards from a drawer and played Go Fish with him. She couldn't concentrate, and Jason quickly grew bored. Unaccustomed to playing without his brother, he asked for an ice pop, a red one, of course, and went to the front porch to wait for Jimmy to wake.

Unable to sit still, she paced from one end of her home to the other, her uneasiness increasing with every step. In desperation, she picked up the phone and tried Conor again. When the secretary told her he was still out of the office, she asked to speak with Mac Pearson.

He came on the line, and Bekka had to hold the phone away from her ear. "Jumpin' catfish, I've been hearing a lot about you! All of it good . . ."

"I need to speak to Conor," she interrupted.

Mac's tone of voice changed. "What's wrong? Are you all right? Your boys?"

Bekka released a shaky breath and murmured, "We're all right. But there's been another fire. Here. Can you tell Conor?"

Suddenly alert, her ears strained to make out an unfamiliar sound. A tormented wail had her slamming the phone down, cutting off Mac's reply. She followed the sound to the family room, where Jimmy cried, his sobs muffled into his pillow. He thrashed about in his sleep, the thin blanket a tangled heap at his feet.

"Dad-dy . . . !" His high-pitched scream chilled her down to her soul.

She took him in her arms and murmured, "Jimmy, I'm here, honey. I'm here."

"Noooo!" he cried.

"You're safe, Jimmy. Mommy's here."

"Daddy. Crashed."

Bekka kissed his forehead, crooning unintelligible words of comfort. After a long silence, he mumbled something she couldn't hear. "What did you say, honey?"

"Daddy. Crashed," he repeated.

Worry prickled down her spine. Could Jimmy really remember the night his father died? He hadn't even been two and a half when it happened. Bekka remembered all the mornings these past few weeks Jimmy's sheets had been pulled out, the nights he'd cried out in his sleep. The first time had been the morning after those teenagers had crashed into the tree in the front yard. Had that crash sparked memories of the other one?

"Do you remember your father, Jimmy?"

"He lit matches. He yelled."

She set him away from her so she could look into his face. Wiping away his tears, she murmured, "Your father lit matches because he smoked. Do you remember that?"

Jimmy shook his head.

He may not remember in his mind, but he had in his dream. "He hated me and Jas."

Bekka closed her eyes against her tears. When she opened them, she brushed a curl from Jimmy's forehead and said, "He didn't hate you, honey. He didn't hate any of us. He just couldn't stay with us. He was intelligent and ambitious, but he couldn't live with the responsibility of a family. He cared for us in his own way, and when he died, he left us enough money to buy this house."

Her sons had been one and two when Ted had died. She doubted they remembered their father's face, but his angry words had come back to haunt them all.

"He hated me."

"No, Jimmy, I promise you, he didn't." She smoothed his curls away from his face before continuing. "In fact, he told me he loved you and Jason. It was the last thing he said before he walked out the door the night he died."

"He loved us?"

"Yes, honey. I didn't know you were watching, didn't know you were there at the window with me, until it was too late. He was sad when he left, and he drove out of the alley without looking. There was an accident. He died a few hours later from an injury to his head. Your father died peacefully. The doctors said he felt no pain."

The child hiccuped in her arms, and a sound drew her gaze to the other side of the room. Tears swam in her eyes, making the man standing in the curved archway appear larger than life.

"I came as soon as I heard."

Managing no more than a hoarse whisper, she said, "That person was here, right outside that door."

Conor came into the room, his gaze riveted to hers. "Did you see or hear anything?"

"Who was here, Mommy?" Jimmy asked.

"Don't worry, Jimmy, you're safe now," she murmured. After a moment she said, "Honey, I need to talk to Conor. Take an ice pop from the freezer and go out to the porch with Jason for a few minutes. Then, if you want, I'll tell you more about your father."

The little boy looked from her face to Conor's, and the look in his eyes made Bekka want to weep. When he left the room, she pushed to her feet and paced to the far side of the room. Turning, she said, "Too much pain. Conor, we've all been through too much pain."

"It's almost over."

"No. You thought it was over twelve years ago. But it wasn't. I thought it was over five years ago. But it isn't. Jimmy just had a nightmare. About his father. I've always worried about him. He's always seemed so vulnerable, and now I know he bears the emotional scars of a father he can't even remember."

"What does that have to do with now?" he asked.

Bekka closed her eyes at the look in his. They'd both seen too much, experienced too much heartache. "God knows you've been through enough, Conor. I can't ask you to take on my problems, too.''

"And if I offered?''

"I can't,'' she whispered. "I can't accept.''

"Conor! Look at me!'' Jason's voice carried on the breeze.

Without another word, Conor turned and strode from her house. He swallowed the despair in his throat and looked on as Jason hopped on his bike, then rode with no hands for all of two seconds.

"Way to go, Jason!'' he called, hoping the child didn't hear the false brightness in his voice.

He sank down to the step, feeling weariness wash over him. He was tired and soul-weary. And why not? He'd been born tired, and the threat of fire these past few weeks had further exhausted him.

He'd finally found what had been missing all his life. It was there in Bekka's smile, in her eyes, and in her heart. She'd offered him everything she had, all her love, all her strength. And now, when she was the one in need, she'd turned away.

He'd always known she was stubborn. She wasn't the only one. He still couldn't risk her safety, and the fact that someone had set a fire right outside her window gnawed at his insides. He had to find Vince. He had to find out who was responsible. Then he'd be back. He'd offer her everything that made him whole, and he wouldn't take no for an answer.

His fatigue vanished, and new hope sprang to life. He pushed himself from the step and strode toward his truck. Jimmy stood on the sidewalk, blocking his path. The ice pop lay on the ground, and the boy's chin was touching his chest, his shoulders shaking.

Kneeling down, Conor let his knees grind into the hard cement. Jimmy sniffled, and Conor realized the child was crying, and he doubted it was because he'd dropped his frozen treat. He gently pulled the boy into his strong embrace. At first Jimmy remained stiff, but after a moment, he buried his curly-topped head into the hollow of Conor's shoulder.

"Jim. What is it?"

"I didn't mean to. Honest I didn't. I heard Mommy tell you that a bad man did it. But he didn't. I did it. I did, Conor."

Fear gripped Conor's heart like a vise. "What did you do, Jimmy?"

"I started the fire on those old boards," the child sobbed.

Conor held him until the sobs died away. Reaching into his back pocket, he pulled out a handkerchief and handed it to Jimmy. Taking the proffered square, the child took a moment to restore his dignity.

"How?" Conor asked.

With a sob and a hiccup, Jimmy stepped out of Conor's embrace. "I was playing with matches. I know I'm not s'posed to. And I won't ever, ever again. I lit one, then another. The fire was pretty, Conor. Then all the matches caught fire and I dropped them. I blew, and I thought they were out. But the wood musta been lit, cuz later it was all on fire."

Conor breathed a huge sigh of relief and suddenly understood what it felt like to be a father. Jimmy hadn't set that fire on purpose. It had been an accident. He'd overheard part of the child's memories of his father, and Conor knew the poor kid had suffered enough. But did Jimmy know that?

"I think you've learned your lesson, Jim. But just to make sure, I want you to help me clean up that mess. Then you can help me wash the soot from the bricks on the garage. And I want you to promise me you'll never play with matches again."

"I promise, Conor."

He ruffled the boy's curls and felt a love he'd never known was possible. Jim placed the soiled handkerchief in Conor's big hand and met his gaze. "Remember when you told me and Jas if you could have chosen a father, you would have chosen Mac?"

"I remember, Jim."

"If I could choose a dad, I'd pick you."

Conor wanted to crush the child to him, to protect him, keep him safe. If he could choose a son, he'd choose Jimmy, and Jason, too. "I'm proud of you, Jim." It was all Conor could do to squeeze the words through a throat that had suddenly closed up. "Feeling better?"

"Yeah," Jimmy declared.

"Feel like riding bikes with Jason?" As the boy skipped off to his bike, Conor's gaze swung around and collided with Bekka's. Even from this distance, he could see unshed tears brightening her eyes and knew she'd heard Jimmy's confession.

He hadn't expected the surge of passion that engulfed him, and his heart swelled with the memory of their lovemaking. For a moment, she remained frozen in the doorway. Then she pushed through and glided down the steps. Conor couldn't reach her fast enough. His arms went around her, and he buried his face in her hair.

He kissed the corner of her eyes and tasted the salt of her tears. Those tears fueled his feelings, and he crushed her to him, covering her mouth with his.

Tires sounded on gravel and the kids' voices called out. "Mommy, Conor, it's the police!"

Conor scowled at the intrusion. He'd rarely been able to kiss her properly without interruption.

Both Bekka and Conor turned their heads as the police car pulled into the driveway. She slid from his embrace but stayed close to his side.

"Bekka. Conor." Vince Macelli, still in uniform, stepped around the front of the car.

Bekka stared wordlessly across at Vince. He looked haggard, as if he hadn't slept in a week. Lines were etched in his face, and his eyes had a burning, faraway look in them. There was something he had to tell Conor, something that would cost him dearly, and she doubted anything she said or did would make it easier.

"If Mac was here, he'd say you look like something the cat dragged in, Macelli," Conor said.

"That's about how I feel."

"Just say it, Vince. Say it and put an end to all this."

"You're right," Vince snapped. "You're right. I . . ."

Bekka held her breath and waited for him to continue.

"I didn't want to believe it. I fought against believing it. And now it's over. My old man hated your father. And he hated you. But most of all, he hated me."

Bekka couldn't stop the tears from streaming down her cheeks.

"But it's over. When I found him this morning, his clothes reeked of gasoline, the gasoline he'd used to douse your new house. I took him to the hospital, but his old lungs had breathed in too much smoke over the years. This last fire was one too many. He died an hour ago. My father's dead, Conor. He admitted he set fire to your new house. It's finally over."

Vince stumbled, and if Conor hadn't been there, he would have fallen to the ground. Bekka swiped at her own tears and held the door as Conor helped Vince inside.

There was no time to brew coffee. Vince needed something now. She made instant and placed a steaming mug before each of them. With her soft-as-a-caress voice, Bekka asked, "Why, Vince? Why did he do it?"

"Because he hated Conor. And he hated Conor's father."

"Conor told me about that night, the night his house burned twelve years ago. He told me about what he saw, what his father did. I understand why your father hated Sam Bradley then, but what happened before that night?"

Vince stared into his mug for a long time before meeting Conor's gaze. "I don't know. But my mother does. She's coming tomorrow. She's arranged for a graveside service, and she wants you to come, Conor."

Without touching his coffee, Vince stood. "I have to go. There are some things I need to take care of."

Conor stood, too, and followed Vince out the door. Bekka stood inside the doorway, her gaze drawn to her sons, who were standing on the sidewalk, their arms draped across each other's shoulders.

Vince murmured something to the boys, and they grinned up at him. "Me and Jas are playing brothers," Jimmy called.

"How do you play that?" Vince asked.

"It's kind of like playing house," Jason answered. "Except there's no girls, no dolls, and no dumb stuff."

Bekka smiled through her tears. Halfway to his car, Vince turned. "It wasn't you I was hitting that night, Conor. It was your old man. I never meant to hurt you."

Conor's back was to her. She couldn't see his expression but saw his shoulders move. "I know, Vince. I've always known."

Vince and Conor stood side by side, Bekka on Conor's right, Gloria Parker on her son's left, the only four people present at the burial. Walter Parker, Gloria's husband, stood down the hill in the background, lending his wife moral support. The service had been simple, the prayer short yet meaningful. There were no flowers, no flowery phrases. The priest shook their hands, offering each of them his heartfelt condolence before he left.

No one said anything for several moments, and the silence grew as thick as water. Vince's mother was a petite brunette with sparkling blue eyes. She hadn't shed a tear, but her voice, when she spoke, was emotion-filled. "Leroy wasn't always filled with hatred. What he tried to do for me was honorable. But his jealousy ate away at the goodness in him."

One by one, they turned and began to walk along the winding cemetery path. For weeks Conor had known Leroy Macelli had started the rumor twelve years ago, the one linking Conor to the fire that destroyed his home. Now he knew Leroy had been at the hospital waiting for a breathing treatment the night Mara had her surgery and had overheard Mike's telephone conversation with Bekka. He knew Leroy had thrown the brick through Bekka's window and the pipe through Conor's. Those things Conor understood. But he still couldn't understand the man's hatred for him.

"If Leroy hated me so much, why did he keep that lot all these years?" Conor asked.

"Leroy didn't keep that lot, Conor. I did."

Three pairs of eyes were suddenly trained on the extraordinary expression in Gloria's gaze. She took a deep breath and smiled at the two men, one her son and the other his best friend. "Leroy wasn't always a monster. When he was young, he was an honorable man. I promised Leroy that, as long as he was alive, I wouldn't tell you boys."

"Tell us what?" Vince asked his mother. "Why in

the world would you pay for Conor's lot all these years?''

"Because I hoped he'd come back to it someday,'' she answered.

Song sparrows and goldfinches called to each other across the wide open land. As Bekka tucked an errant strand of hair behind her ear, a new feeling of peace began to take root in her. There was a reason Gloria Macelli Parker had wanted Conor to come back to Millerton. Looking at Vince and Conor, both strong, both tall, both dark, she saw that reason was becoming clear.

"Leroy and Sam were always rivals,'' Gloria said. "It didn't matter if it was motorcycles, cars, or women, they always tried to outdo each other. Leroy loved me in his own way, but I was just a girl, and there was something about the look in Sam's eyes that drew me. I knew his reputation with the girls, but that one time, it didn't matter. I thought Sam loved me. I thought I could tame the wildness in him. But I was wrong. The next day he'd taken up with another girl.'' She turned to Conor. "Your mother.''

"To make a long story short, I married Leroy, and Sam married your mother, Conor, seven months before you were born. Leroy married me because, you see, I was pregnant, too. But Leroy wasn't the father.''

Vince stared at his mother. Conor stared at Vince. And Bekka gazed at them both. "Vince, you and Conor are half-brothers,'' Gloria whispered.

"Brothers,'' Bekka echoed, tears streaming freely down her face.

Gloria implored them with her look and with her next question. "Do you have any idea how difficult it was to know you were half-brothers, and not be able to tell you? If anyone needed a brother, it was the two of you. But I promised Leroy when he married me, and I promised him again eighteen years later when he saved me from Sam.''

Conor stared into Vince's eyes, silence growing tight with tension. For a moment, his brain refused to believe what his ears had heard. Sam Bradley, Conor's father, was Vince's father, too. No wonder Leroy hadn't wanted Conor around. He'd been a constant reminder that Vince wasn't *his* son. Leroy had done the honorable thing and married the girl he'd loved. But he hadn't been strong enough, and his jealousy and hatred had shrunk that love until it withered away to nothing.

Brothers whispered through Conor's mind, floated through his chest. It didn't matter that they were actually half-brothers. The half was simply a technicality. Conor and Vince were brothers, in the true sense of the word.

Neither man was comfortable with open displays of affection, neither knew how to demonstrate what he was feeling. They continued to look at each other, their tension evaporating like dew in the sun. Conor's hands slid to his hips, Vince's delved deep into his pockets.

"Brothers," Vince declared.

One corner of Conor's mouth twitched, and one by one, his features became animated. Laughter floated up from his throat, marvelous, catching. Bekka slipped her hands around his waist, half laughing, half crying.

Vince hugged his mother, then the women switched, Bekka hugging Vince, Gloria hugging Conor. Before they knew it, they were all a tangle of arms and jackets. Vince sputtered, "What the hell," and grasped Conor in a stiff hug.

It was over as quickly as it began. Gloria sniffed, and Bekka beamed. They'd reached the cars where Walter Parker clasped Vince's shoulder. "Let's go home," he murmured.

With arms entwined, Bekka and Conor watched as

Vince slid into the backseat. He turned, and his gaze swung to theirs. Bekka looked from one man to the other. Warmth settled to her heart as, for the first time in twelve years, they smiled at each other without reservation.

The car pulled away, and Conor drew her into his embrace. His kiss was a promise, and she answered on a sigh. Looking into his deep blue eyes, she whispered, "The fires are over, Conor. Now we can go home."

The look in his eyes warmed her. His lips touched hers, and another kind of warmth filled her. Love. The house fires were over, but the fire that burned in their hearts would continue to warm them, would continue to draw them together. Forever.

With hands clasped, they walked over the winding cement path to Conor's Chevy. Bekka kissed him before climbing inside and again before he started the engine. She gazed into his eyes, the same eyes she'd become lost in twelve years ago. That night a bond had been formed. Today, that bond had grown as strong and sturdy as bricks.

Conor ground the lever into first and covered her hand with his own. She'd smiled at him a long time ago. He returned that smile now. He placed her hand beneath his on the shifting lever, where it stayed as they turned toward the country and headed home.

EPILOGUE

"You may kiss the bride."

Conor's hands slid around Bekka's waist, his work-roughened palms rasping over ice-blue taffeta. He lowered his face to hers, his smile slow and secret, a smile she understood. The gold band on her finger sparkled in the sunshine as she brought her hand to his cheek. Her other hand slid up the smooth fabric on his jacket as warmth and happiness filled her senses.

His kiss sang through her veins as Jason's voice sang through the air. "They're at it again!"

Their lips clung, then parted on their laughter. Conor rested his forehead against hers, groaning deep in his throat. He was getting used to having his kisses interrupted.

There were hugs all around, and back slaps, and tears, and more laughter. Conor bent down. Sliding a hand beneath each of them, he swung both boys into his arms. A camera captured the moment before Jimmy and Jason giggled and wiggled to be put down, embarrassed and proud and secure.

Guests assembled in groups throughout the backyard,

beneath streamers blowing in the breeze. Green apples glinted from every branch of the tree, more fragrant than any flowers. Bekka and Conor sipped champagne and cut their wedding cake. They talked to every guest, but their gazes never strayed far from each other.

"Look at me, Uncle Vince!" Jason called, and all eyes turned to the apple tree where several children were playing.

Gloria Parker wiped a tear from her eye because the child had called her son "Uncle," and Bekka's older brother muttered, "That's not a tree house. It's a tree condo. Those two will be spoiled rotten within the year."

Emma Taylor shook her finger at her firstborn and admonished, "There's a difference between being loved and being spoiled, Todd. I wouldn't say anything if I were you, at least not until after your baby's born."

Todd slid his arm around Tammy's waist, or at least as far as he could reach. "How's our little Taylor Taylor?" he asked loud enough for everyone to hear. Tammy jabbed him in the ribs, and Frank Taylor threw his hands into the air.

Mac Pearson slapped Conor on the back, commenting on the progress he and Vince were making on the house. Conor had tried to give the lot to Vince, but the stubborn man wouldn't hear of it. He insisted on buying it, and the house they were building together was turning into a beauty.

"Bek," Mara cut in. "I have the perfect match for Vince . . ."

Bekka listened with only one ear, her eyes following Conor and the boys across the back of the lot. She'd known she'd loved Conor, had known he loved her, too. But she'd never believed it was possible to be this happy.

Mara's conversation forced Bekka's thoughts to the

wedding reception. To her credit, Mara hadn't complained, not even once, about having the wedding outside, the ceremony near the apple tree in Vince's lot. She'd taken over the preparations, of course, and had overseen even the smallest detail.

". . . After all, I've given up on Dustin. I've run out of women whose names begin with the letter *d*." With that, Mara dashed off and scooped up her son, righting the punch bowl the second before he could pull the tablecloth out from beneath it.

"Beautiful weddin'," Bud Trierweller mumbled.

Bekka smiled at him, murmuring her thanks. To his grandson, she said, "Part of the praise goes to you, Randy. You've done a beautiful job with this yard." The fourteen-year-old blushed two shades of red, but the smile on his face was as proud as the punch little Marc had nearly spilled.

Conor caught up with Bekka under the apple tree, where he bent to kiss his wife. Their lips met dreamily, then parted. Their eyes opened, and Conor's heart lurched at the loving glow in her gaze. He reacted to the look in her eyes, to the warm smile on her lips. His clothes suddenly felt too tight. Loosening his tie didn't help.

"This is the best tree house," Jason piped from over their heads. Vince smiled at them from beneath the apple tree, and Bekka felt her heart swell to nearly bursting. Several of the guests had already left, and Bekka wanted to do the same.

"Let's go home," she whispered with a knowing smile.

Conor's voice, when he spoke, was a degree deeper than normal. "Jim, Jas, it's time to go home."

"Okay, Daddy," Jason answered.

Jimmy jumped from the last rung. Taking Conor's

large hand in his small one, he said, "Come on, Dad. Let's go home."

Jason scrambled to take Bekka's hand, and the four of them turned. Rice pattered down on them and, with hands clasped, they all lowered their chins and started to run.

Their laughter rang through the air. Breathless, they squeezed inside Conor's Chevy, which was decorated with streamers and balloons and tin cans. Waving to all their favorite people, they pulled away from the curb.

With love glowing in their eyes and in their hearts, Bekka and Conor and Jim and Jas went home.

SHARE THE FUN . . .
SHARE YOUR NEW-FOUND TREASURE!!

You don't want to let your new books out of your sight? That's okay. Your friends can get their own. Order below.

No. 90 HOLD BACK THE NIGHT by Sandra Steffen
Shane is a man with a mission and ready for anything . . . except Starr.

No. 145 UNTIL TOMORROW by Sandra Steffen
Bekka wanted to know the truth about Conor but he wasn't about to tell.

No. 77 FLIGHT OF THE SWAN by Lacey Dancer
Rich had decided to swear off romance for good until Christiana.

No. 78 TO LOVE A COWBOY by Laura Phillips
Dee is the dark-haired beauty that sends Nick reeling back to the past.

No. 79 SASSY LADY by Becky Barker
No matter how hard he tries, Curt can't seem to get away from Maggie.

No. 80 CRITIC'S CHOICE by Kathleen Yapp
Marlis can't do one thing right in front of her handsome houseguest.

No. 81 TUNE IN TOMORROW by Laura Michaels
Deke happily gave up life in the fast lane. Can Liz do the same?

No. 82 CALL BACK OUR YESTERDAYS by Phyllis Houseman
Michael comes to terms with his past with Laura by his side.

No. 83 ECHOES by Nancy Morse
Cathy comes home and finds love even better the second time around.

No. 84 FAIR WINDS by Helen Carras
Fate blows Eve into Vic's life and he finds he can't let her go.

No. 85 ONE SNOWY NIGHT by Ellen Moore
Randy catches Scarlett fever and he finds there's no cure.

No. 86 MAVERICK'S LADY by Linda Jenkins
Bentley considered herself worldly but she was not prepared for Reid.

No. 87 ALL THROUGH THE HOUSE by Janice Bartlett
Abigail is just doing her job but Nate blocks her every move.

No. 88 MORE THAN A MEMORY by Lois Faye Dyer
Cole and Melanie both still burn from the heat of that long ago summer.

No. 89 JUST ONE KISS by Carole Dean
Michael is Nikki's guardian angel and too handsome for his own good.

No. 91 FIRST MATE by Susan Macias
It only takes a minute for Mac to see that Amy isn't so little anymore.

No. 92 TO LOVE AGAIN by Dana Lynn Hites
Cord thought just one kiss would be enough. But Honey proved him wrong!

No. 93 NO LIMIT TO LOVE by Kate Freiman
Lisa was called the "little boss" and Bruiser didn't like it one bit!

No. 94 SPECIAL EFFECTS by Jo Leigh
Catlin wouldn't fall for any tricks from Luke, the master of illusion.

No. 96 THERE IS A SEASON by Phyllis Houseman
The heat of the volcano rivaled the passion between Joshua and Beth.

No. 97 THE STILLMAN CURSE by Peggy Morse
Leandra thought revenge would be sweet. Todd had sweeter things in mind.

No. 98 BABY MAKES FIVE by Lacey Dancer
Cait could say 'no' to his business offer but not to Robert, the man.

No. 99 MOON SHOWERS by Laura Phillips
Both Sam and the historic Missouri home quickly won Hilary's heart.

No. 100 GARDEN OF FANTASY by Karen Rose Smith
If Beth wasn't careful, she'd fall into the arms of her enemy, Nash.

Meteor Publishing Corporation
Dept. 593, P. O. Box 41820, Philadelphia, PA 19101-9828

Please send the books I've indicated below. Check or money order (U.S. Dollars only)—no cash, stamps or C.O.D.s (PA residents, add 6% sales tax). I am enclosing $2.95 plus 75¢ handling fee for *each* book ordered.

Total Amount Enclosed: $_____.

____ No. 90	____ No. 81	____ No. 87	____ No. 94
____ No. 145	____ No. 82	____ No. 88	____ No. 96
____ No. 77	____ No. 83	____ No. 89	____ No. 97
____ No. 78	____ No. 84	____ No. 91	____ No. 98
____ No. 79	____ No. 85	____ No. 92	____ No. 99
____ No. 80	____ No. 86	____ No. 93	____ No. 100

Please Print:
Name _____
Address _____ Apt. No. _____
City/State _____ Zip _____

Allow four to six weeks for delivery. Quantities limited.

fire chief spoke to Red Enetrother, to other neighbors, to Cotter, and to Wince. The firemen rolled up their